Adventures In Contentment

David Grayson

Contents

ADVENTURES IN CONTENTMENT

BY

David Grayson

I
"THE BURDEN OF THE VALLEY OF VISION"

I came here eight years ago as the renter of this farm, of which soon afterward I became the owner. The time before that I like to forget. The chief impression it left, upon my memory, now happily growing indistinct, is of being hurried faster than I could well travel. From the moment, as a boy of seventeen, I first began to pay my own way, my days were ordered by an inscrutable power which drove me hourly to my task. I was rarely allowed to look up or down, but always forward, toward that vague Success which we Americans love to glorify.

My senses, my nerves, even my muscles were continually strained to the utmost of attainment. If I loitered or paused by the wayside, as it seems natural for me to do, I soon heard the sharp crack of the lash. For many years, and I can say it truthfully, I never rested. I neither thought nor reflected. I had no pleasure, even though I pursued it fiercely during the brief respite of vacations. Through many feverish years I did not work: I merely produced.

The only real thing I did was to hurry as though every moment were my last, as though the world, which now seems so rich in everything, held only one prize which might be seized upon before I arrived. Since then I have tried to recall, like one who struggles to restore the visions of a fever, what it was that I ran to attain, or why I should have borne without rebellion such indignities to soul and body. That life seems now, of all illusions, the most distant and unreal. It is like the unguessed eternity before we are born: not of concern compared with that eternity upon which we are now embarked.

All these things happened in cities and among crowds. I like to forget them. They smack of that slavery of the spirit which is so much worse than any mere slavery of the body.

One day--it was in April, I remember, and the soft maples in the city park were just beginning to blossom--I stopped suddenly. I did not intend to stop. I confess in humiliation that it was no courage, no will of my own. I intended to go on toward Success: but Fate stopped me. It was as if I had been thrown violently from a moving planet: all the universe streamed around me and past me. It seemed to me that of all animate creation, I was the only thing that was still or silent. Until I stopped I had not known the pace I ran; and I had a vague sympathy and understanding, never felt before, for those who left the running. I lay prostrate with fever and close to death for weeks and watched the world go by: the dust, the noise, the very colour of haste. The only sharp pang that I suffered was the feeling that I should be broken-hearted and that I was not; that I should care and that I did not. It was as though I had died and escaped all further responsibility. I even watched with dim equanimity my friends racing past me, panting as they ran. Some of them paused an instant to comfort me where I lay, but I could see that their minds were still upon the running and I was glad when they went away. I cannot tell with what weariness their haste oppressed me. As for them, they somehow blamed me for dropping out. I knew. Until we ourselves understand, we accept no excuse from the man who stops. While I felt it all, I was not bitter. I did not seem to care. I said to myself: "This is Unfitness. I survive no longer. So be it."

Thus I lay, and presently I began to hunger and thirst. Desire rose within me: the indescribable longing of the convalescent for the food of recovery. So I lay, questioning wearily what it was that I required. One morning I wakened with a strange, new joy in my soul. It came to me at that moment with indescribable poignancy, the thought of walking barefoot in cool, fresh plow furrows as I had once done when a boy. So vividly the memory came to me--the high airy world as it was at that moment, and the boy I was walking free in the furrows--that the weak tears filled my eyes, the first I had shed in many years. Then I thought of sitting in quiet thickets in old fence corners, the wood behind me rising still, cool, mysterious, and the fields in front stretching away in illimitable pleasantness. I thought of the good smell of cows at milking--you do not know, if you do not know!--I thought of the sights and sounds, the heat and sweat of the hay fields. I thought of a certain brook I knew when a boy that flowed among alders and wild parsnips, where I waded with a three-foot rod for trout. I thought of all these things as a man thinks of his first love. Oh, I craved the soil. I hungered and thirsted for the earth. I was greedy for growing things.

And thus, eight years ago, I came here like one sore-wounded creeping from the field of battle. I remember walking in the sunshine, weak yet, but curiously satisfied. I that was dead lived again. It came to me then with a curious certainty, not since so assuring, that I understood the chief marvel of nature hidden within the Story of the Resurrection, the marvel of plant and seed, father and son, the wonder of the seasons, the miracle of life. I, too, had died: I had lain long in darkness, and now I had risen again upon the sweet earth. And I possessed beyond others a knowledge of a former existence, which I knew, even then, I could never return to.

For a time, in the new life, I was happy to drunkenness--working, eating, sleeping. I was an animal again, let out to run in green pastures. I was glad of the sunrise and the sunset. I was glad at noon. It delighted me when my muscles ached with work and when, after supper, I could not keep my eyes open for sheer weariness. And sometimes I was awakened in the night out of a sound sleep--seemingly by the very silences--and lay in a sort of bodily comfort impossible to describe.

I did not want to feel or to think: I merely wanted to live. In the sun or the rain I wanted to go out and come in, and never again know the pain of the unquiet spirit. I looked forward to an awakening not without dread for we are as helpless before birth as in the presence of death.

But like all birth, it came, at last, suddenly. All that summer I had worked in a sort of animal content. Autumn had now come, late autumn, with coolness in the evening air. I was plowing in my upper field--not then mine in fact--and it was a soft afternoon with the earth turning up moist and fragrant. I had been walking the furrows all day long. I had taken note, as though my life depended upon it, of the occasional stones or roots in my field, I made sure of the adjustment of the harness, I drove with peculiar care to save the horses. With such simple details of the work in hand I had found it my joy to occupy my mind. Up to that moment the most important things in the world had seemed a straight furrow and well-turned corners--to me, then, a profound accomplishment.

I cannot well describe it, save by the analogy of an opening door somewhere within the house of my consciousness. I had been in the dark: I seemed to emerge. I had been bound down: I seemed to leap up--and with a marvellous sudden sense of freedom and joy.

I stopped there in my field and looked up. And it was as if I had never looked up before. I discovered another world. It had been there before, for long and long, but I had never seen nor felt it. All discoveries are made in that way: a man finds the new thing, not in nature but in himself.

It was as though, concerned with plow and harness and furrow, I had never known that the world had height or colour or sweet sounds, or that there was *feeling* in a hillside. I forgot myself, or where I was. I stood a long time motionless. My dominant feeling, if I can at all express it, was of a strange new friendliness, a warmth, as though these hills, this field about me, the woods, had suddenly spoken to me and caressed me. It was as though I had been accepted in membership, as though I was now recognised, after long trial, as belonging here.

Across the town road which separates my farm from my nearest neighbour's, I saw a field, familiar, yet strangely new and unfamiliar, lying up to the setting sun, all red with autumn, above it the incalculable heights of the sky, blue, but not quite clear, owing to the Indian summer haze. I cannot convey the sweetness and softness of that landscape, the airiness of it, the mystery of it, as it came to me at that moment. It was as though, looking at an acquaintance long known, I should discover that I loved him. As I stood there I was conscious of the cool tang of burning leaves and brush heaps, the lazy smoke of which floated down the long valley and found me in my field, and finally I heard, as though the sounds were then made for the first time, all the vague murmurs of the country side--a cow-bell somewhere in the distance, the creak of a wagon, the blurred evening hum of birds, insects, frogs. So much it means for a man to stop and look up from his task. So I stood, and I looked up and down with a glow and a thrill which I cannot now look back upon without some envy and a little amusement at the very grandness and seriousness of it all. And I said aloud to myself:

"I will be as broad as the earth. I will not be limited."

Thus I was born into the present world, and here I continue, not knowing what other world I may yet achieve. I do not know, but I wait in expectancy, keeping my furrows straight and my corners well turned. Since that day in the field, though my fences include no more acres, and I still plow my own fields, my real domain has expanded until I crop wide fields and take the profit of many curious pastures.

From my farm I can see most of the world; and if I wait here long enough all people pass this way.

And I look out upon them not in the surroundings which they have chosen for themselves, but from the vantage ground of my familiar world. The symbols which meant so much in cities mean little here. Sometimes it seems to me as though I saw men naked. They come and stand beside my oak, and the oak passes solemn judgment; they tread my furrows and the clods give silent evidence; they touch the green blades of my corn, the corn whispers its sure conclusions. Stern judgments that will be deceived by no symbols!

Thus I have delighted, secretly, in calling myself an unlimited farmer, and I make this confession in answer to the inner and truthful demand of the soul that we are not, after all, the slaves of things, whether corn, or banknotes, or spindles; that we are not the used, but the users; that life is more than profit and loss. And so I shall expect that while I am talking farm some of you may be thinking dry goods, banking, literature, carpentry, or what-not. But if you can say: I am an unlimited dry goods merchant, I am an unlimited carpenter, I will give you an old-fashioned country hand-shake, strong and warm. We are friends; our orbits coincide.

II
I BUY A FARM

As I have said, when I came here I came as a renter, working all of the first summer without that "open vision" of which the prophet Samuel speaks. I had no memory of the past and no hope of the future. I fed upon the moment. My sister Harriet kept the house and I looked after the farm and the fields. In all those months I hardly knew that I had neighbours, although Horace, from whom I rented my place, was not infrequently a visitor. He has since said that I looked at him as though he were a "statute." I was "citified," Horace said; and "citified" with us here in the country is nearly the limit of invective, though not violent enough to discourage such a gift of sociability as his. The Scotch Preacher, the rarest, kindest man I know, called once or twice, wearing the air of formality which so ill becomes him. I saw nothing in him: it was my fault, not his, that I missed so many weeks of his friendship. Once in that time the Professor crossed my fields with his tin box slung from his shoulder; and the only feeling I had, born of crowded cities, was that this was an intrusion upon my property. Intrusion: and the Professor! It is now unthinkable. I often passed the Carpentry Shop on my way to town. I saw Baxter many times at his bench. Even then Baxter's eyes attracted me: he always glanced up at me as I passed, and his look had in it something of a caress. So the home of Starkweather, standing aloof among its broad lawns and tall trees, carried no meaning for me.

Of all my neighbours, Horace is the nearest. From the back door of my house, looking over the hill, I can see the two red chimneys of his home, and the top of the windmill. Horace's barn and corn silo are more pretentious by far than his house, but fortunately they stand on lower ground, where they are not visible from my side of the hill. Five minutes' walk in a straight line across the fields brings me to

Horace's door; by the road it takes at least ten minutes.

In the fall after my arrival I had come to love the farm and its surroundings so much that I decided to have it for my own. I did not look ahead to being a farmer. I did not ask Harriet's advice. I found myself sitting one day in the justice's office. The justice was bald and as dry as corn fodder in March. He sat with spectacled impressiveness behind his ink-stained table. Horace hitched his heel on the round of his chair and put his hat on his knee. He wore his best coat and his hair was brushed in deference to the occasion. He looked uncomfortable, but important. I sat opposite him, somewhat overwhelmed by the business in hand. I felt like an inadequate boy measured against solemnities too large for him. The processes seemed curiously unconvincing, like a game in which the important part is to keep from laughing; and yet when I thought of laughing I felt cold chills of horror. If I had laughed at that moment I cannot think what that justice would have said! But it was a pleasure to have the old man read the deed, looking at me over his spectacles from time to time to make sure I was not playing truant. There are good and great words in a deed. One of them I brought away with me from the conference, a very fine, big one, which I love to have out now and again to remind me of the really serious things of life. It gives me a peculiar dry, legal feeling. If I am about to enter upon a serious bargain, like the sale of a cow, I am more avaricious if I work with it under my tongue.

Hereditaments! Hereditaments!

Some words need to be fenced in, pig-tight, so that they cannot escape us; others we prefer to have running at large, indefinite but inclusive. I would not look up that word for anything: I might find it fenced in so that it could not mean to me all that it does now.

Hereditaments! May there be many of them--or it!

Is it not a fine Providence that gives us different things to love? In the purchase of my farm both Horace and I got the better of the bargain--and yet neither was cheated. In reality a fairly strong lantern light will shine through Horace, and I could see that he was hugging himself with the joy of his bargain; but I was content. I had some money left--what more does anyone want after a bargain?--and I had come into possession of the thing I desired most of all. Looking at bargains from a purely commercial point of view, someone is always cheated, but looked at with the simple eye both seller and buyer always win.

We came away from the gravity of that bargaining in Horace's wagon. On our way home Horace gave me fatherly advice about using my farm. He spoke from the height of his knowledge to me, a humble beginner. The conversation ran something like this:

HORACE: Thar's a clump of plum trees along the lower pasture fence. Perhaps you saw 'm----

MYSELF: I saw them: that is one reason I bought the back pasture. In May they will be full of blossoms.

HORACE: They're *wild* plums: they ain't good for nothing.

MYSELF: But think how fine they will be all the year round.

HORACE: Fine! They take up a quarter-acre of good land. I've been going to cut 'em myself this ten years.

MYSELF: I don't think I shall want them cut out.

HORACE: Humph.

After a pause:

HORACE: There's a lot of good body cord-wood in that oak on the knoll.

MYSELF: Cord-wood! Why, that oak is the treasure of the whole farm, I have never seen a finer one. I could not think of cutting it.

HORACE: It will bring you fifteen or twenty dollars cash in hand.

MYSELF: But I rather have the oak.

HORACE: Humph.

So our conversation continued for some time. I let Horace know that I preferred rail fences, even old ones, to a wire fence, and that I thought a farm should not be too large, else it might keep one away from his friends. And what, I asked, is corn compared with a friend? Oh, I grew really oratorical! I gave it as my opinion that there should be vines around the house (Waste of time, said Horace), and that no farmer should permit anyone to paint medicine advertisements on his barn (Brings you ten dollars a year, said Horace), and that I proposed to fix the bridge on the lower road (What's a path-master for? asked Horace). I said that a town was a useful adjunct for a farm; but I laid it down as a principle that no town should be too near a farm. I finally became so enthusiastic in setting forth my conceptions of a true farm that I reduced Horace to a series of humphs. The early humphs were incredulous, but as I proceeded, with some joy, they became humorously contemptuous, and finally began to voice a large, comfortable, condescending tolerance. I could fairly feel Horace growing superior as he sat there beside me. Oh, he had everything in his favour. He could prove what he said: One tree + one thicket = twenty dollars. One landscape = ten cords of wood = a quarter-acre of corn = twenty dollars. These equations prove themselves. Moreover, was not Horace the "best off" of any farmer in the country? Did he not have the largest barn and the best corn silo? And are there better arguments?

Have you ever had anyone give you up as hopeless? And is it not a pleasure? It is only after people resign you to your fate that you really make friends of them. For how can you win the friendship of one who is trying to convert you to his superior beliefs?

As we talked, then, Horace and I, I began to have hopes of him. There is no joy comparable to the making of a friend, and the more resistant the material the greater the triumph. Baxter, the carpenter, says that when he works for enjoyment he chooses curly maple.

When Horace set me down at my gate that afternoon he gave me his hand and told me that he would look in on me occasionally, and that if I had any trouble to let him know.

A few days later I heard by the roundabout telegraph common in country neighbourhoods that Horace had found a good deal of fun in reporting what I said about farming and that he had called me by a highly humorous but disparaging name. Horace has a vein of humour all his own. I have caught him alone in his fields chuckling to himself, and even breaking out in a loud laugh at the memory of some amusing incident that happened ten years ago. One day, a month or more after our bargain, Horace came down across his field and hitched his jean-clad leg over my fence, with the intent, I am sure, of delving a little more in the same rich mine of humour.

"Horace," I said, looking him straight in the eye, "did you call me an--Agriculturist!"

I have rarely seen a man so pitifully confused as Horace was at that moment. He flushed, he stammered, he coughed, the perspiration broke out on his forehead. He tried to speak and could not. I was sorry for him.

"Horace," I said, "you're a Farmer."

We looked at each other a moment with dreadful seriousness, and then both of us laughed to the point of holding our sides. We slapped our knees, we shouted, we wriggled, we almost rolled with merriment. Horace put out his hand and we shook heartily. In five minutes I had the whole story of his humorous reports out of him.

No real friendship is ever made without an initial clashing which discloses the metal of each to each. Since that day Horace's jean-clad leg has rested many a time on my fence and we have talked crops and calves. We have been the best of friends in the way of whiffle-trees, butter tubs and pig killings--but never once looked up together at the sky.

The chief objection to a joke in the country is that it is so imperishable. There is so much room for jokes and so few jokes to fill it. When I see Horace approaching with a peculiar, friendly, reminiscent smile on his face I hasten with all ardour to anticipate him:

"Horace," I exclaim, "you're a Farmer."

III

THE JOY OF POSSESSION

How sweet the west wind sounds in my own trees: How graceful climb these shadows on my hill."

Always as I travel, I think, "Here I am, let anything happen!"

I do not want to know the future; knowledge is too certain, too cold, too real.

It is true that I have not always met the fine adventure nor won the friend, but if I had, what should I have more to look for at other turnings and other hilltops?

The afternoon of my purchase was one of the great afternoons of my life. When Horace put me down at my gate, I did not go at once to the house; I did not wish, then, to talk with Harriet. The things I had with myself were too important. I skulked toward my barn, compelling myself to walk slowly until I reached the corner, where I broke into an eager run as though the old Nick himself were after me. Behind the barn I dropped down on the grass, panting with laughter, and not without some of the shame a man feels at being a boy. Close along the side of the barn, as I sat there in the cool of the shade, I could see a tangled mat of smartweed and catnip, and the boards of the barn, brown and weather-beaten, and the gables above with mud swallows' nests, now deserted; and it struck me suddenly, as I observed these homely pleasant things:

"All this is mine."

I sprang up and drew a long breath.

"Mine," I said.

It came to me then like an inspiration that I might now go out and take formal possession of my farm. I might experience the emotion of a landowner. I might swell with dignity and importance--for once, at least.

So I started at the fence corner back of the barn and walked straight up through the pasture, keeping close to my boundaries, that I might not miss a single rod of my acres. And oh, it was a prime afternoon! The Lord made it! Sunshine--and autumn haze--and red trees--and yellow fields--and blue distances above the far-away town. And the air had a tang which got into a man's blood and set him chanting all the poetry he ever knew.

"I climb that was a clod,   I run whose steps were slow, I reap the very wheat of God   That once had none to sow!"

So I walked up the margin of my field looking broadly about me: and presently, I began to examine my fences-- *my* fences--with a critical eye. I considered the quality of the soil, though in truth I was not much of a judge of such matters. I gloated over my plowed land, lying there open and passive in the sunshine. I said of this tree: "It is mine," and of its companion beyond the fence: "It is my neighbour's." Deeply and sharply within myself I drew the line between *meum* and *tuum*: for only thus, by comparing ourselves with our neighbours, can we come to the true realisation of property. Occasionally I stopped to pick up a stone and cast it over the fence, thinking with some truculence that my neighbour would probably throw it back again. Never mind, I had it out of *my* field. Once, with eager surplusage of energy, I pulled down a dead and partly rotten oak stub, long an eye-sore, with an important feeling of proprietorship. I could do anything I liked. The farm was *mine*.

How sweet an emotion is possession! What charm is inherent in ownership! What a foundation for vanity, even for the greater quality of self-respect, lies in a little property! I fell to thinking of the excellent wording of the old books in which land is called "real property," or "real estate." Money we may possess, or goods or chattels, but they give no such impression of mineness as the feeling that one's feet rest upon soil that is his: that part of the deep earth is his with all the water upon it, all small animals that creep or crawl in the holes of it, all birds or insects that fly in the air above it, all trees, shrubs, flowers, and grass that grow upon it, all houses, barns and fences--all, his. As I strode along that afternoon I fed upon possession. I rolled the sweet morsel of ownership under my tongue. I seemed to set my feet down more firmly on the good earth. I straightened my shoulders: *this land was mine*. I picked up a clod of earth and let it crumble and drop through my fingers: it gave me a peculiar and poignant feeling of possession. I can understand why the miser enjoys the very physical contact of his gold. Every sense I possessed, sight, hearing, smell, touch, led upon the new joy.

At one corner of my upper field the fence crosses an abrupt ravine upon leggy stilts. My line skirts the slope halfway up. My neighbour owns the crown of the hill which he has shorn until it resembles the tonsured pate of a monk. Every rain brings the light soil down the ravine and lays it like a hand of infertility upon my farm. It had always bothered me, this wastage; and as I looked across my fence I thought to myself:

"I must have that hill. I will buy it. I will set the fence farther up. I will plant the slope. It is no age of tonsures either in religion or agriculture."

The very vision of widened acres set my thoughts on fire. In imagination I extended my farm upon all sides, thinking how much better I could handle my land than my neighbours. I dwelt avariciously upon more possessions: I thought with discontent of my poverty. More land I wanted. I was enveloped in clouds of envy. I coveted my neighbour's land: I felt myself superior and Horace inferior: I was consumed with black vanity.

So I dealt hotly with these thoughts until I reached the top of the ridge at the farther corner of my land. It is the highest point on the farm.

For a moment I stood looking about me on a wonderful prospect of serene beauty. As it came to me--hills, fields, woods--the fever which had been consuming me died down. I thought how the world stretched away from my fences--just such fields--for a thousand miles, and in each small enclosure a man as hot as I with the passion of possession. How they all envied, and hated, in their longing for more land! How property kept them apart, prevented the close, confident touch of friendship, how it separated lovers and ruined families! Of all obstacles to that complete democracy of which we dream, is there a greater than property?

I was ashamed. Deep shame covered me. How little of the earth, after all, I said, lies within the limits of my fences. And I looked out upon the perfect beauty of the world around me, and I saw how little excited it was, how placid, how undemanding.

I had come here to be free and already this farm, which I thought of so fondly as my possession, was coming to possess me. Ownership is an appetite like hunger or thirst, and as we may eat to gluttony and drink to drunkenness so we may possess to avarice. How many men have I seen who, though they regard themselves as models of temperance, wear the marks of unbridled indulgence of the passion of possession, and how like gluttony or licentiousness it sets its sure sign upon their faces.

I said to myself, Why should any man fence himself in? And why hope to enlarge one's world by the creeping acquisition of a few acres to his farm? I thought of the old scientist, who, laying his hand upon the grass, remarked: "Everything under my hand is a miracle"--forgetting that everything outside was also a miracle.

As I stood there I glanced across the broad valley wherein lies the most of my farm, to a field of buckwheat which belongs to Horace. For an instant it gave me the illusion of a hill on fire: for the late sun shone full on the thick ripe stalks of the buckwheat, giving forth an abundant red glory that blessed the eye. Horace had been proud of his crop, smacking his lips at the prospect of winter pancakes, and here I was entering his field and taking without hindrance another crop, a crop gathered not with hands nor stored in granaries: a wonderful crop, which, once gathered, may long be fed upon and yet remain unconsumed.

So I looked across the countryside; a group of elms here, a tufted hilltop there, the smooth verdure of pastures, the rich brown of new-plowed fields--and the odours, and the sounds of the country--all cropped by me. How little the fences keep me out: I do not regard titles, nor consider boundaries. I enter either by day or by night, but not secretly. Taking my fill, I leave as much as I find.

And thus standing upon the highest hill in my upper pasture, I thought of the quoted saying of a certain old abbot of the middle ages--"He that is a true monk considers nothing as belonging to him except a lyre."

What finer spirit? Who shall step forth freer than he who goes with nothing save his lyre? He shall sing as he goes: he shall not be held down nor fenced in.

With a lifting of the soul I thought of that old abbot, how smooth his brow, how catholic his interest, how serene his outlook, how free his friendships, how unlimited his whole life. Nothing but a lyre!

So I made a covenant there with myself. I said: "I shall use, not be used. I do not limit myself here. I shall not allow possessions to come between me and my life or my friends."

For a time--how long I do not know--I stood thinking. Presently I discovered, moving slowly along the margin of the field below me, the old professor with his tin botany box. And somehow I had no feeling that he was intruding upon my new land. His walk was slow and methodical, his head and even his shoulders were bent--almost habitually--from looking close upon the earth, and from time to time he stooped, and once he knelt to examine some object that attracted his eye. It seemed appropriate that he should thus kneel to the earth. So he gathered *his* crop and fences did not keep him out nor titles disturb him. He also was free! It gave me at that moment a peculiar pleasure to have him on my land, to know that I was, if unconsciously, raising other crops than I knew. I felt friendship for this old professor: I could understand him, I thought. And I said aloud but in a low tone, as though I were addressing him:

--Do not apologise, friend, when you come into my field. You do not interrupt me. What you have come for is of more importance at this moment than corn. Who is it that says I must plow so many furrows this day? Come in, friend, and sit here on these clods: we will sweeten the evening with fine words. We will invest our time not in corn, or in cash, but in life.--

I walked with confidence down the hill toward the professor. So engrossed was he with his employment that he did not see me until I was within a few paces of him. When he looked up at me it was as though his eyes returned from some far journey. I felt at first out of focus, unplaced, and only gradually coming into view. In his hand he held a lump of earth containing a thrifty young plant of the purple cone-flower, having several blossoms. He worked at the lump deftly, delicately, so that the earth, pinched, powdered and shaken out, fell between his fingers, leaving the knotty yellow roots in his hand. I marked how firm, slow, brown, the old man was, how little obtrusive in my field. One foot rested in a furrow, the other was set among the grass of the margin, near the fence--his place, I thought.

His first words, though of little moment in themselves, gave me a curious satisfaction, as when a coin, tested, rings true gold, or a hero, tried, is heroic.

"I have rarely," he said, "seen a finer display of rudbeckia than this, along these old fences."

If he had referred to me, or questioned, or apologised, I should have been disappointed. He did not say, "your fences," he said "these fences," as though they were as much his as mine. And he spoke in his own world, knowing that if I could enter I would, but that if I could not, no stooping to me would avail either of us.

"It has been a good autumn for flowers," I said inanely, for so many things were flying through my mind that I could not at once think of the great particular words which should bring us together. At first I thought my chance had passed, but he seemed to see something in me after all, for he said:

"Here is a peculiarly large specimen of the rudbeckia. Observe the deep purple of the cone, and the bright yellow of the petals. Here is another that grew hardly two feet away, in the grass near the fence where the rails and the blackberry bushes have shaded it. How small and undeveloped it is."

"They crowd up to the plowed land," I observed.

"Yes, they reach out for a better chance in life--like men. With more room, better food, freer air, you see how much finer they grow."

It was curious to me, having hitherto barely observed the cone-flowers along my fences, save as a colour of beauty, how simply we fell to talking of them as though in truth they were people like ourselves, having our desires and possessed of our capabilities. It gave me then, for the first time, the feeling which has since meant such varied enjoyment, of the peopling of the woods.

"See here," he said, "how different the character of these individuals. They are all of the same species. They all grow along this fence within two or three rods; but observe the difference not only in size but in colouring, in the shape of the petals, in the proportions of the cone. What does it all mean? Why, nature trying one of her endless experiments. She sows here broadly, trying to produce better cone-flowers. A few she plants on the edge of the field in the hope that they may escape the plow. If they grow, better food and more sunshine produce more and larger flowers."

So we talked, or rather he talked, finding in me an eager listener. And what he called botany seemed to me to be life. Of birth, of growth, of reproduction, of death, he spoke, and his flowers became sentient creatures under my eyes.

And thus the sun went down and the purple mists crept silently along the distant low spots, and all the great, great mysteries came and stood before me beckoning and questioning. They came and they stood, and out of the cone-flower, as the old professor spoke, I seemed to catch a glimmer of the true light. I reflected how truly everything is in anything. If one could really understand a cone-flower he could understand this Earth. Botany was only one road toward the Explanation.

Always I hope that some traveller may have more news of the way than I, and sooner or later, I find I must make inquiry of the direction of every thoughtful man I meet. And I have always had especial hope of those who study the sciences: they ask such intimate questions of nature. Theology possesses a vain-gloriousness which places its faith in human theories; but science, at its best, is humble before nature herself. It has no thesis to defend: it is content to kneel upon the earth, in the way of my friend, the old professor, and ask the simplest questions, hoping for some true reply.

I wondered, then, what the professor thought, after his years of work, of the Mystery; and finally, not without confusion, I asked him. He listened, for the first time ceasing to dig, shake out and arrange his specimens. When I had stopped speaking he remained for a moment silent, then he looked at me with a new regard. Finally he quoted quietly, but with a deep note in his voice:

"Canst thou by searching find God? Canst thou find out the Almighty unto perfection? It is as high as heaven: what canst thou do? deeper than hell, what canst thou know?"

When the professor had spoken we stood for a moment silent, then he smiled and said briskly:

"I have been a botanist for fifty-four years. When I was a boy I believed implicitly in God. I prayed to him, having a vision of him--a person--before my eyes. As I grew older I concluded that there was no God. I dismissed him from the universe. I believed only in what I could see, or hear, or feel. I talked about Nature and Reality."

He paused, the smile still lighting his face, evidently recalling to himself the old days. I did not interrupt him. Finally he turned to me and said abruptly.

"And now--it seems to me--there is nothing but God."

As he said this he lifted his arm with a peculiar gesture that seemed to take in the whole world.

For a time we were both silent. When I left him I offered my hand and told him I hoped I might become his friend. So I turned my face toward home. Evening was falling, and as I walked I heard the crows calling, and the air was keen and cool, and I thought deep thoughts.

And so I stepped into the darkened stable. I could not see the outlines of the horse or the cow, but knowing the place so well I could easily get about. I heard the horse step aside with a soft expectant whinny. I smelled the smell of milk, the musty, sharp odour of dry hay, the pungent smell of manure, not unpleasant. And the stable was warm after the cool of the fields with a sort of animal warmth that struck into me soothingly. I spoke in a low voice and laid my hand on the horse's flank. The flesh quivered and shrunk away from my touch--coming back confidently, warmly. I ran my hand along his back and up his hairy neck. I felt his sensitive nose in my hand. "You shall have your oats," I said, and I gave him to eat. Then I spoke as gently to the cow, and she stood aside to be milked.

And afterward I came out into the clear bright night, and the air was sweet and cool, and my dog came bounding to meet me.--So I carried the milk into the house, and Harriet said in her heartiest tone:

"You are late, David. But sit up, I have kept the biscuits warm."

And that night my sleep was sound.

IV
ENTERTAIN AN AGENT UNAWARES

With the coming of winter I thought the life of a farmer might lose something of its charm. So much interest lies in the growth not only of crops but of trees, vines, flowers, sentiments and emotions. In the summer the world is busy, concerned with many things and full of gossip: in the winter I anticipated a cessation of many active interests and enthusiasms. I looked forward to having time for my books and for the quiet contemplation of the life around me. Summer indeed is for activity, winter for reflection. But when winter really came every day discovered some new work to do or some new adventure to enjoy. It is surprising how many things happen on a small farm. Examining the book which accounts for that winter, I find the history of part of a forenoon, which will illustrate one of the curious adventures of a farmer's life. It is dated January 5.

*   *   *   *   *

I went out this morning with my axe and hammer to mend the fence along the public road. A heavy frost fell last night and the brown grass and the dry ruts of the roads were powdered white. Even the air, which was perfectly still, seemed full of frost crystals, so that when the sun came up one seemed to walk in a magic world. I drew in a long breath and looked out across the wonderful shining country and I said to myself:

"Surely, there is nowhere I would rather be than here." For I could have travelled nowhere to find greater beauty or a better enjoyment of it than I had here at home.

As I worked with my axe and hammer, I heard a light wagon come rattling up the road. Across the valley a man had begun to chop a tree. I could see the axe steel flash brilliantly in the sunshine before I heard the sound of the blow.

The man in the wagon had a round face and a sharp blue eye. I thought he seemed a businesslike young man.

"Say, there," he shouted, drawing up at my gate, "would you mind holding my horse a minute? It's a cold morning and he's restless."

"Certainly not," I said, and I put down my tools and held his horse.

He walked up to my door with a brisk step and a certain jaunty poise of the head.

"He is well contented with himself," I said. "It is a great blessing for any man to be satisfied with what he has got."

I heard Harriet open the door--how every sound rang through the still morning air!

The young man asked some question and I distinctly heard Harriet's answer: "He's down there."

The young man came back: his hat was tipped up, his quick eye darted over my grounds as though in a single instant he had appraised everything and passed judgment upon the cash value of the inhabitants. He whistled a lively little tune.

"Say," he said, when he reached the gate, not at all disconcerted, "I thought you was the hired man. Your name's Grayson, ain't it? Well, I want to talk with you."

After tying and blanketing his horse and taking a black satchel from his buggy he led me up to my house. I had a pleasurable sense of excitement and adventure. Here was a new character come to my farm. Who knows, I thought, what he may bring with him: who knows what I may send away by him? Here in the country we must set our little ships afloat on small streams, hoping that somehow, some day, they will reach the sea.

It was interesting to see the busy young man sit down so confidently in our best chair. He said his name was Dixon, and he took out from his satchel a book with a fine showy cover. He said it was called "Living Selections from Poet, Sage and Humourist."

"This," he told me, "is only the first of the series. We publish six volumes full of literchoor. You see what a heavy book this is?"

I tested it in my hand: it was a heavy book.

"The entire set," he said, "weighs over ten pounds. There are 1,162 pages, enough paper if laid down flat, end to end, to reach half a mile."

I cannot quote his exact language: there was too much of it, but he made an impressive showing of the amount of literature that could be had at a very low price per pound. Mr. Dixon was a hypnotist. He fixed me with his glittering eye, and he talked so fast, and his ideas upon the subject were so original that he held me spellbound. At first I was inclined to be provoked: one does not like to be forcibly hypnotised, but gradually the situation began to amuse me, the more so when Harriet came in.

"Did you ever see a more beautiful binding?" asked the agent, holding his book admiringly at arm's length. "This up here," he said, pointing to the illuminated cover, "is the Muse of Poetry She is scattering flowers--poems, you know. Fine idea, ain't it? Colouring fine, too."

He jumped up quickly and laid the book on my table, to the evident distress of Harriet.

"Trims up the room, don't it?" he exclaimed, turning his head a little to one side and observing the effect with an expression of affectionate admiration.

"How much," I asked, "will you sell the covers for without the insides?"

"Without the insides?"

"Yes," I said, "the binding will trim up my table just as well without the insides."

I thought he looked at me a little suspiciously, but he was evidently satisfied by my expression of countenance, for he answered promptly:

"Oh, but you want the insides. That's what the books are for. The bindings are never sold alone."

He then went on to tell me the prices and terms of payment, until it really seemed that it would be cheaper to buy the books than to let him carry them away again. Harriet stood in the doorway behind him frowning and evidently trying to catch my eye. But I kept my face turned aside so that I could not see her signal of distress and my eyes fixed on the young man Dixon. It was as good as a play. Harriet there, serious-minded, thinking I was being befooled, and the agent thinking he was befooling me, and I, thinking I was befooling both of them--and all of us wrong. It was very like life wherever you find it.

Finally, I took the book which he had been urging upon me, at which Harriet coughed meaningly to attract my attention. She knew the danger when I really got my hands on a book. But I made up as innocent as a child. I opened the book almost at random--and it was as though, walking down a strange road, I had come upon an old tried friend not seen before in years. For there on the page before me I read:

"The world is too much with us; late and soon, Getting and spending we lay waste our powers: Little we see in Nature that is ours; We have given our hearts away, a sordid boon! The sea that bares her bosom to the moon; The winds that will be howling at all hours, But are up-gathered now like sleeping flowers; For this, for everything, we are out of tune; It moves us not."

And as I read it came back to me--a scene like a picture--the place, the time, the very feel of the hour when I first saw those lines. Who shall say that the past does not live! An odour will sometimes set the blood coursing in an old emotion, and a line of poetry is the resurrection and the life. For a moment I forgot Harriet and the agent, I forgot myself, I even forgot the book on my knee--everything but that hour in the past--a view of shimmering hot housetops, the heat and dust and noise of an August evening in the city, the dumb weariness of it all, the loneliness, the longing for green fields; and then these great lines of Wordsworth, read for the first time, flooding in upon me:

"Great God! I'd rather be A pagan suckled in a creed outworn: So might I, standing on this pleasant lea, Have glimpses that would make me less forlorn; Have sight of Proteus rising from the sea; And hear old Triton blow his wreathed horn."

When I had finished I found myself standing in my own room with one arm raised, and, I suspect, a trace of tears in my eyes--there before the agent and Harriet. I saw Harriet lift one hand and drop it hopelessly. She thought I was captured at last. I was past saving. And as I looked at the agent I saw "grim conquest glowing in his eye!" So I sat down not a little embarrassed by my exhibition--when I had intended to be self-poised.

"You like it, don't you?" said Mr. Dixon unctuously.

"I don't see," I said earnestly, "how you can afford to sell such things as this so cheap."

"They *are* cheap," he admitted regretfully. I suppose he wished he had tried me with the half-morocco.

"They are priceless," I said, "absolutely priceless. If you were the only man in the world who had that poem, I think I would deed you my farm for it."

Mr. Dixon proceeded, as though it were all settled, to get out his black order book and open it briskly for business. He drew his fountain pen, capped it, and looked up at me expectantly. My feet actually seemed slipping into some irresistible whirlpool. How well he understood practical psychology! I struggled within myself, fearing engulfment: I was all but lost.

"Shall I deliver the set at once," he said, "or can you wait until the first of February?"

At that critical moment a floating spar of an idea swept my way and I seized upon it as the last hope of the lost.

"I don't understand," I said, as though I had not heard his last question, "how you dare go about with all this treasure upon you. Are you not afraid of being stopped in the road and robbed? Why, I've seen the time when, if I had known you carried such things as these, such cures for sick hearts, I think I should have stopped you myself!"

"Say, you *are* an odd one," said Mr. Dixon.

"Why do you sell such priceless things as these?" I asked, looking at him sharply.

"Why do I sell them?" and he looked still more perplexed. "To make money, of course; same reason you raise corn."

"But here is wealth," I said, pursuing my advantage. "If you have these you have something more valuable than money."

Mr. Dixon politely said nothing. Like a wise angler, having failed to land me at the first rush, he let me have line. Then I thought of Ruskin's words, "Nor can any noble thing be wealth except to a noble person." And that prompted me to say to Mr. Dixon:

"These things are not yours; they are mine. You never owned them; but I will sell them to you."

He looked at me in amazement, and then glanced around--evidently to discover if there were a convenient way of escape.

"You're all straight, are you?" he asked tapping his forehead; "didn't anybody ever try to take you up?"

"The covers are yours," I continued as though I had not heard him, "the insides are mine and have been for a long time: that is why I proposed buying the covers separately."

I opened his book again. I thought I would see what had been chosen for its pages. And I found there many fine and great things.

"Let me read you this," I said to Mr. Dixon; "it has been mine for a long time. I will not sell it to you. I will give it to you outright. The best things are always given."

Having some gift in imitating the Scotch dialect, I read:

"November chill blaws loud wi' angry sugh;   The shortening winter day is near a close; The miry beasts retreating frae the pleugh;   The black'ning trains o' craws to their repose: The toil-worn Cotter frae his labour goes,   This night his weekly moil is at an end,   Collects his spades, his mattocks and his hoes,   Hoping the morn in ease and rest to spend,   And weary, o'er the moor, his course does hameward bend."

So I read "The Cotter's Saturday Night." I love the poem very much myself, sometimes reading it aloud, not so much for the tenderness of its message, though I prize that, too, as for the wonder of its music:

"Compared with these, Italian trills are tame;   The tickl'd ear no heart-felt raptures raise."

I suppose I showed my feeling in my voice. As I glanced up from time to time I saw the agent's face change, and his look deepen and the lips, usually so energetically tense, loosen with emotion. Surely no poem in all the language conveys so perfectly the simple love of the home, the quiet joys, hopes, pathos of those who live close to the soil.

When I had finished--I stopped with the stanza beginning:

"Then homeward all take off their sev'ral way";

the agent turned away his head trying to brave out his emotion. Most of us, Anglo-Saxons, tremble before a tear when we might fearlessly beard a tiger.

I moved up nearer to the agent and put my hand on his knee; then I read two or three of the other things I found in his wonderful book. And once I had him laughing and once again I had the tears in his eyes. Oh, a simple young man, a little crusty without, but soft inside--like the rest of us.

Well, it was amazing once we began talking not of books but of life, how really eloquent and human he became. From being a distant and uncomfortable person, he became at once like a near neighbour and friend. It was strange to me--as I have thought since--how he conveyed to us in few words the essential emotional note of his life. It was no violin tone, beautifully complex with harmonics, but the clear simple voice of the flute. It spoke of his wife and his baby girl and his home. The very incongruity of detail--he told us how he grew onions in his back yard--added somehow to the homely glamour of the vision which he gave us. The number of his house, the fact that he had a new cottage organ, and that the baby ran away and lost herself in Seventeenth Street--were all, curiously, fabrics of his emotion.

It was beautiful to see commonplace facts grow phosphorescent in the heat of true feeling. How little we may come to know Romance by the cloak she wears and how humble must be he who would surprise the heart of her!

It was, indeed, with an indescribable thrill that I heard him add the details, one by one--the mortgage on his place, now rapidly being paid off, the brother who was a plumber, the mother-in-law who was not a mother-in-law of the comic papers. And finally he showed us the picture of the wife and baby that he had in the cover of his watch; a fat baby with its head resting on its mother's shoulder.

"Mister," he said, "p'raps you think it's fun to ride around the country like I do, and be away from home most of the time. But it ain't. When I think of Minnie and the kid--"

He broke off sharply, as if he had suddenly remembered the shame of such confidences.

"Say," he asked, "what page is that poem on?"

I told him.

"One forty-six," he said. "When I get home I'm going to read that to Minnie. She likes poetry and all such things. And where's that other piece that tells how a man feels when he's lonesome? Say, that fellow knew!"

We had a genuinely good time, the agent and I, and when he finally rose to go, I said:

"Well, I've sold you a new book."

"I see now, mister, what you mean."

I went down the path with him and began to unhitch his horse.

"Let me, let me," he said eagerly.

Then he shook hands, paused a moment awkwardly as if about to say something, then sprang into his buggy without saying it.

When he had taken up his reins he remarked:

"Say! but you'd make an agent! You'd hypnotise 'em."

I recognised it as the greatest compliment he could pay me: the craft compliment.

Then he drove off, but pulled up before he had gone five yards. He turned in his seat, one hand on the back of it, his whip raised.

"Say!" he shouted, and when I walked up he looked at me with fine embarrassment.

"Mister, perhaps you'd accept one of these sets from Dixon free gratis, for nothing."

"I understand," I said, "but you know I'm giving the books to you--and I couldn't take them back again."

"Well," he said, "you're a good one, anyhow. Good-bye again," and then, suddenly, business naturally coming uppermost, he remarked with great enthusiasm:

"You've given me a new idea. *Say*, I'll sell 'em."

"Carry them carefully, man," I called after him; "they are precious."

So I went back to my work, thinking how many fine people there are in this world--if you scratch 'em deep enough.

V
THE AXE-HELVE

April the 15th.

This morning I broke my old axe handle. I went out early while the fog still filled the valley and the air was cool and moist as it had come fresh from the filter of the night. I drew a long breath and let my axe fall with all the force I could give it upon a new oak log. I swung it unnecessarily high for the joy of doing it and when it struck it communicated a sharp yet not unpleasant sting to the palms of my hands. The handle broke short off at the point where the helve meets the steel. The blade was driven deep in the oak wood. I suppose I should have regretted my foolishness, but I did not. The handle was old and somewhat worn, and the accident gave me an indefinable satisfaction: the culmination of use, that final destruction which is the complement of great effort.

This feeling was also partly prompted by the thought of the new helve I already had in store, awaiting just such a catastrophe. Having come somewhat painfully by that helve, I really wanted to see it in use.

Last spring, walking in my fields, I looked out along the fences for a well-fitted young hickory tree of thrifty second growth, bare of knots at least head high, without the cracks or fissures of too rapid growth or the doziness of early transgression. What I desired was a fine, healthy tree fitted for a great purpose and I looked for it as I would look for a perfect man to save a failing cause. At last I found a sapling growing in one of the sheltered angles of my rail fence. It was set about by dry grass, overhung by a much larger cherry tree, and bearing still its withered last year's leaves, worn diaphanous but curled delicately, and of a most beautiful ash gray colour, something like the fabric of a wasp's nest, only yellower. I gave it a shake and it sprung quickly under my hand like the muscle of a good horse. Its bark was smooth and trim, its bole well set and solid.

A perfect tree! So I came up again with my short axe and after clearing away the grass and leaves with which the wind had mulched it, I cut into the clean white roots. I had no twinge of compunction, for was this not fulfillment? Nothing comes of sorrow for worthy sacrifice. When I had laid the tree low, I clipped off the lower branches, snapped off the top with a single clean stroke of the axe, and shouldered as pretty a second-growth sapling stick as anyone ever laid his eyes upon.

I carried it down to my barn and put it on the open rafters over the cow stalls. A cow stable is warm and not too dry, so that a hickory log cures slowly without cracking or checking. There it lay for many weeks. Often I cast my eyes up at it with satisfaction, watching the bark shrink and slightly deepen in colour, and once I climbed up where I could see the minute seams making way in the end of the stick.

In the summer I brought the stick into the house, and put it in the dry, warm storeroom over the kitchen where I keep my seed corn. I do not suppose it really needed further attention, but sometimes when I chanced to go into the storeroom, I turned it over with my foot. I felt a sort of satisfaction in knowing that it was in preparation for service: good material for useful work. So it lay during the autumn and far into the winter.

One cold night when I sat comfortably at my fireplace, listening to the wind outside, and feeling all the ease of a man at peace with himself, my mind took flight to my snowy field sides and I thought of the trees there waiting and resting through the winter. So I came in imagination to the particular corner in the fence where I had cut my hickory sapling. Instantly I started up, much to Harriet's astonishment, and made my way mysteriously up the kitchen stairs. I would not tell what I was after: I felt it a sort of adventure, almost like the joy of seeing a friend long forgotten. It was as if my hickory stick had cried out at last, after long chrysalishood:

"I am ready."

I stood it on end and struck it sharply with my knuckles: it rang out with a certain clear resonance.

"I am ready."

I sniffed at the end of it. It exhaled a peculiar good smell, as of old fields in the autumn.

"I am ready."

So I took it under my arm and carried it down.

"Mercy, what are you going to do?" exclaimed Harriet.

"Deliberately, and with malice aforethought," I responded, "I am going to litter up your floor. I have decided to be reckless. I don't care what happens."

Having made this declaration, which Harriet received with becoming disdain, I laid the log by the fireplace--not too near--and went to fetch a saw, a hammer, a small wedge, and a draw-shave.

I split my log into as fine white sections as a man ever saw--every piece as straight as morality, and without so much as a sliver to mar it. Nothing is so satisfactory as to have a task come out in perfect time and in good order. The little pieces of bark and sawdust I swept scrupulously into the fireplace, looking up from time to time to see how Harriet was taking it. Harriet was still disdainful.

Making an axe-helve is like writing a poem (though I never wrote one). The material is free enough, but it takes a poet to use it. Some people imagine that any fine thought is poetry, but there was never a greater mistake. A fine thought, to become poetry, must be seasoned in the upper warm garrets of the mind for long and long, then it must be brought down and slowly carved into words, shaped with emotion, polished with love. Else it is no true poem. Some people imagine that any hickory stick will make an axe-helve. But this is far from the truth. When I had whittled away for several evenings with my draw-shave and jack-knife, both of which I keep sharpened to the keenest edge, I found that my work was not progressing as well as I had hoped.

"This is more of a task," I remarked one evening, "than I had imagined."

Harriet, rocking placidly in her arm-chair, was mending a number of pairs of new socks, Poor Harriet! Lacking enough old holes to occupy her energies, she mends holes that may possibly appear. A frugal person!

"Well, David," she said, "I warned you that you could buy a helve cheaper than you could make it."

"So I can buy a book cheaper than I can write it," I responded.

I felt somewhat pleased with my return shot, though I took pains not to show it. I squinted along my hickory stick which was even then beginning to assume, rudely, the outlines of an axe-handle. I had made a prodigious pile of fine white shavings and I was tired, but quite suddenly there came over me a sort of love for that length of wood. I sprung it affectionately over my knee, I rubbed it up and down with my hand, and then I set it in the corner behind the fireplace.

"After all," I said, for I had really been disturbed by Harriet's remark--"after all, power over one thing gives us power over everything. When you mend socks prospectively--into futurity--Harriet, that is an evidence of true greatness."

"Sometimes I think it doesn't pay," remarked Harriet, though she was plainly pleased.

"Pretty good socks," I said, "can be bought for fifteen cents a pair."

Harriet looked at me suspiciously, but I was as sober as the face of nature.

For the next two or three evenings I let the axe-helve stand alone in the corner. I hardly looked at it, though once in a while, when occupied with some other work, I would remember, or rather half remember, that I had a pleasure in store for the evening. The very thought of sharp tools and something, to make with them acts upon the imagination with peculiar zest. So we love to employ the keen edge of the mind upon a knotty and difficult subject.

One evening the Scotch preacher came in. We love him very much, though he sometimes makes us laugh--perhaps, in part, because he makes us laugh. Externally he is a sort of human cocoanut, rough, brown, shaggy, but within he has the true milk of human kindness. Some of his qualities touch greatness. His youth was spent in stony places where strong winds blew; the trees where he grew bore thorns; the soil where he dug was full of roots. But the crop was human love. He possesses that quality, unusual in one bred exclusively in the country, of magnanimity toward the unlike. In the country we are tempted to throw stones at strange hats! But to the Scotch preacher every man in one way seems transparent to the soul. He sees the man himself, not his professions any more than his clothes. And I never knew anyone who had such an abiding disbelief in the wickedness of the human soul. Weakness he sees and comforts; wickedness he cannot see.

When he came in I was busy whittling my axe-helve, it being my pleasure at that moment to make long, thin, curly shavings so light that many of them were caught on the hearth and bowled by the draught straight to fiery destruction.

There is a noisy zest about the Scotch preacher: he comes in "stomping" as we say, he must clear his throat, he must strike his hands together; he even seems noisy when he unwinds the thick red tippet which he wears wound many times around his neck. It takes him a long time to unwind it, and he accomplishes the task with many slow gyrations of his enormous rough head. When he sits down he takes merely the edge of the chair, spreads his stout legs apart, sits as straight as a post, and blows his nose with a noise like the falling of a tree.

His interest in everything is prodigious. When he saw what I was doing he launched at once upon an account of the methods of axe-helving, ancient and modern, with true incidents of his childhood.

"Man," he exclaimed, "you've clean forgotten one of the preenciple refinements of the art. When you chop, which hand do you hold down?"

At the moment, I couldn't have told "to save my life, so we both got up on our feet and tried.

"It's the right hand down," I decided; "that's natural to me."

"You're a normal right-handed chopper, then," said the Scotch preacher, "as I was thinking. Now let me instruct you in the art. Being right-handed, your helve must bow out--so. No first-class chopper uses a straight handle."

He fell to explaining, with gusto, the mysteries of the bowed handle, and as I listened I felt a new and peculiar interest in my task This was a final perfection to be accomplished, the finality of technique!

So we sat with our heads together talking helves and axes, axes with single blades and axes with double blades, and hand axes and great choppers' axes, and the science of felling trees, with the true philosophy of the last chip, and arguments as to the best procedure when a log begins to "pinch"--until a listener would have thought that the art of the chopper included the whole philosophy of existence--as indeed it does, if you look at it in that way. Finally I rushed out and brought in my old axe-handle, and we set upon it like true artists, with critical proscription for being a trivial product of machinery.

"Man," exclaimed the preacher, "it has no character. Now your helve here, being the vision of your brain and work of your hands, will interpret the thought of your heart."

Before the Scotch preacher had finished his disquisition upon the art of helve-making and its relations with all other arts, I felt like Peary discovering the Pole.

In the midst of the discourse, while I was soaring high, the Scotch preacher suddenly stopped, sat up, and struck his knee with a tremendous resounding smack.

"Spoons!" he exclaimed.

Harriet and I stopped and looked at him in astonishment.

"Spoons," repeated Harriet.

"Spoons," said the Scotch preacher. "I've not once thought of my errand; and my wife told me to come straight home. I'm more thoughtless every day!"

Then he turned to Harriet:

"I've been sent to borrow some spoons," he said.

"Spoons!" exclaimed Harriet.

"Spoons," answered the Scotch preacher. "We've invited friends for dinner to-morrow, and we must have spoons."

"But why--how--I thought--" began Harriet, still in astonishment.

The Scotch preacher squared around toward her and cleared his throat.

"It's the baptisms," he said: "when a baby is brought for baptism, of course it must have a baptismal gift. What is the best gift for a baby? A spoon. So we present it with a spoon. To-day we discovered we had only three spoons left, and company coming. Man, 'tis a proleefic neighbourhood."

He heaved a great sigh.

Harriet rushed out and made up a package. When she came in I thought it seemed suspiciously large for spoons, but the Scotch preacher having again launched into the lore of the chopper, took it without at first perceiving anything strange. Five minutes after we had closed the door upon him he suddenly returned holding up the package.

"This is an uncommonly heavy package," he remarked; "did I say table-spoons?"

"Go on!" commanded Harriet; "your wife will understand."

"All right--good-bye again," and his sturdy figure soon disappeared in the dark.

"The impractical man!" exclaimed Harriet. "People impose on him."

"What was in that package, Harriet?"

"Oh, I put in a few jars of jelly and a cake of honey."

After a moment Harriet looked up from her work.

"Do you know the greatest sorrow of the Scotch preacher and his wife?"

"What is it?" I asked.

"They have no chick nor child of their own," said Harriet.

It is prodigious, the amount of work required to make a good axe-helve--I mean to make it according to one's standard. I had times of humorous discouragement and times of high elation when it seemed to me I could not work fast enough. Weeks passed when I did not touch the helve but left it standing quietly in the corner. Once or twice I took it out and walked about with it as a sort of cane, much to the secret amusement, I think, of Harriet. At times Harriet takes a really wicked delight in her superiority.

Early one morning in March the dawn came with a roaring wind, sleety snow drove down over the hill, the house creaked and complained in every clapboard. A blind of one of the upper windows, wrenched loose from its fastenings, was driven shut with such force that it broke a window pane. When I rushed up to discover the meaning of the clatter and to repair the damage, I found the floor covered with peculiar long fragments of glass--the pane having been broken inward from the centre.

"Just what I have wanted," I said to myself.

I selected a few of the best pieces and so eager was I to try them that I got out my axe-helve before breakfast and sat scratching away when Harriet came down.

Nothing equals a bit of broken glass for putting on the final perfect touch to a work of art like an axe-helve. Nothing will so beautifully and delicately trim out the curves of the throat or give a smoother turn to the waist. So with care and an indescribable affection, I added the final touches, trimming the helve until it exactly fitted my hand. Often and often I tried it in pantomime, swinging nobly in the centre of the sitting-room (avoiding the lamp), attentive to the feel of my hand as it ran along the helve. I rubbed it down with fine sandpaper until it fairly shone with whiteness. Then I borrowed a red flannel cloth of Harriet and having added a few drops--not too much--of boiled oil, I rubbed the helve for all I was worth. This I continued for upward of an hour. At that time the axe-helve had taken on a yellowish shade, very clear and beautiful.

I do not think I could have been prouder if I had carved a statue or built a parthenon. I was consumed with vanity; but I set the new helve in the corner with the appearance of utter unconcern.

"There," I remarked, "it's finished."

I watched Harriet out of the corner of my eye: she made as if to speak and then held silent.

That evening friend Horace came in. I was glad to see him. Horace is or was a famous chopper. I placed him at the fireplace where his eye, sooner or later, must fall upon my axe-helve. Oh, I worked out my designs! Presently he saw the helve, picked it up at once and turned it over in his hands. I had a suffocating, not unhumorous, sense of self-consciousness. I know how a poet must feel at hearing his first poem read aloud by some other person who does not know its authorship. I suffer and thrill with the novelist who sees a stranger purchase his book in a book-shop. I felt as though I stood that moment before the Great Judge.

Horace "hefted" it and balanced it, and squinted along it; he rubbed it with his thumb, he rested one end of it on the floor and sprung it roughly.

"David," he said severely, "where did you git this?"

Once when I was a boy I came home with my hair wet. My father asked:

"David, have you been swimming?"

I had exactly the same feeling when Horace asked his question. Now I am, generally speaking, a truthful man. I have written a good deal about the immorality, the unwisdom, the short-sightedness, the sinful wastefulness of a lie. But at that moment, if Harriet had not been present--and that illustrates one of the purposes of society, to bolster up a man's morals--I should have evolved as large and perfect a prevarication as it lay within me to do--cheerfully. But I felt Harriet's moral eye upon me: I was a coward as well as a sinner. I faltered so long that Horace finally looked around at me.

Horace has no poetry in his soul, neither does he understand the philosophy of imperfection nor the art of irregularity.

It is a tender shoot, easily blasted by cold winds, the creative instinct: but persistent. It has many adventitious buds. A late frost destroying the freshness of its early verdure, may be the means of a richer growth in later and more favourable days.

*   *   *   *   *

For a week I left my helve standing there in the corner. I did not even look at it. I was slain. I even thought of getting up in the night and putting the helve on the coals--secretly. Then, suddenly, one morning, I took it up not at all tenderly, indeed with a humorous appreciation of my own absurdities, and carried it out into the yard. An axe-helve is not a mere ornament but a thing of sober purpose. The test, after all, of axe-helves is not sublime perfection, but service. We may easily find flaws in the verse of the master--how far the rhythm fails of the final perfect music, how often uncertain the rhyme--but it bears within it, hidden yet evident, that certain incalculable fire which kindles and will continue to kindle the souls of men. The final test is not the perfection of precedent, not regularity, but life, spirit.

It was one of those perfect, sunny, calm mornings that sometimes come in early April: the zest of winter yet in the air, but a promise of summer.

I built a fire of oak chips in the middle of the yard, between two flat stones. I brought out my old axe, and when the fire had burned down somewhat, leaving a foundation of hot coals, I thrust the eye of the axe into the fire. The blade rested on one of the flat stones, and I kept it covered with wet rags in order that it might not heat sufficiently to destroy the temper of the steel. Harriet's old gray hen, a garrulous fowl, came and stood on one leg and looked at me first with one eye and then with the other. She asked innumerable impertinent questions and was generally disagreeable.

"I am sorry, madam," I said finally, "but I have grown adamant to criticism. I have done my work as well as it lies in me to do it. It is the part of sanity to throw it aside without compunction. A work must prove itself. Shoo!"

I said this with such conclusiveness and vigour that the critical old hen departed hastily with ruffled feathers.

So I sat there in the glorious perfection of the forenoon, the great day open around me, a few small clouds abroad in the highest sky, and all the earth radiant with sunshine. The last snow of winter was gone, the sap ran in the trees, the cows fed further afield.

When the eye of the axe was sufficiently expanded by the heat I drew it quickly from the fire and drove home the helve which I had already whittled down to the exact size. I had a hickory wedge prepared, and it was the work of ten seconds to drive it into the cleft at the lower end of the helve until the eye of the axe was completely and perfectly filled. Upon cooling the steel shrunk upon the wood, clasping it with such firmness that nothing short of fire could ever dislodge it. Then, carefully, with knife and sandpaper I polished off the wood around the steel of the axe until I had made as good a job of it as lay within my power.

So I carried the axe to my log-pile. I swung it above my head and the feel of it was good in my hands. The blade struck deep into the oak wood. And I said to myself with satisfaction:

"It serves the purpose."

VI
THE MARSH DITCH

If the day and the night are such that you greet them with joy and life emits a fragrance like flowers and sweet-smelling herbs--is more elastic, more starry, more immortal--that is your Success."

In all the days of my life I have never been so well content as I am this spring. Last summer I thought I was happy, the fall gave me a finality of satisfaction, the winter imparted perspective, but spring conveys a wholly new sense of life, a quickening the like of which I never before experienced. It seems to me that everything in the world is more interesting, more vital, more significant. I feel like "waving aside all roofs," in the way of Le Sage's Asmodeus.

I even cease to fear Mrs. Horace, who is quite the most formidable person in this neighbourhood. She is so avaricious in the saving of souls--and so covetous of mine, which I wish especially to retain. When I see her coming across the hill I feel like running and hiding, and if I were as bold as a boy, I should do it, but being a grown-up coward I remain and dissemble.

She came over this morning. When I beheld her afar off, I drew a long breath: "One thousand," I quoted to myself, "shall flee at the rebuke of one."

In calmness I waited. She came with colours flying and hurled her biblical lance. When I withstood the shock with unexpected jauntiness, for I usually fall dead at once, she looked at me with severity and said:

"Mr. Grayson, you are a materialist."

"You have shot me with a name," I replied. "I am unhurt."

It would be impossible to slay me on a day like this. On a day like this I am immortal.

It comes to me as the wonder of wonders, these spring days, how surely everything, spiritual as well as material, proceeds out of the earth. I have times of sheer Paganism when I could bow and touch my face to the warm bare soil. We are so often ashamed of the Earth--the soil of it, the sweat of it, the good common coarseness of it. To us in our fine raiment and soft manners, it seems indelicate. Instead of seeking that association with the earth which is the renewal of life, we devise ourselves distant palaces and seek strange pleasures. How often and sadly we repeat the life story of the yellow dodder of the moist lanes of my lower farm. It springs up fresh and clean from the earth itself, and spreads its clinging viny stems over the hospitable wild balsam and golden rod. In a week's time, having reached the warm sunshine of the upper air, it forgets its humble beginnings. Its roots wither swiftly and die out, but the sickly yellow stems continue to flourish and spread, drawing their nourishment not from the soil itself, but by strangling and sucking the life juices of the hosts on which it feeds. I have seen whole byways covered thus with yellow dodder--rootless, leafless, parasitic--reaching up to the sunlight, quite cutting off and smothering the plants which gave it life. A week or two it flourishes and then most of it perishes miserably. So many of us come to be like that: so much of our civilization is like that. Men and women there are--the pity of it--who, eating plentifully, have never themselves taken a mouthful from the earth. They have never known a moment's real life of their own. Lying up to the sun in warmth and comfort--but leafless--they do not think of the hosts under them, smothered, strangled, starved. They take *nothing* at first hand. They experience described emotion, and think prepared thoughts. They live not in life, but in printed reports of life. They gather the odour of odours, not the odour itself: they do not hear, they overhear. A poor, sad, second-rate existence!

Bring out your social remedies! They will fail, they will fail, every one, until each man has his feet somewhere upon the soil!

My wild plum trees grow in the coarse earth, among excrementitious mould, a physical life which finally blossoms and exhales its perfect odour: which ultimately bears the seed of its immortality.

Human happiness is the true odour of growth, the sweet exhalation of work: and the seed of human immortality is borne secretly within the coarse and mortal husk. So many of us crave the odour without cultivating the earthly growth from which it proceeds: so many, wasting mortality, expect immortality!

----"Why," asks Charles Baxter, "do you always put the end of your stories first?"

"You may be thankful," I replied, "that I do not make my remarks all endings. Endings are so much more interesting than beginnings."

Without looking up from the buggy he was mending, Charles Baxter intimated that my way had at least one advantage: one always knew, he said, that I really had an end in view--and hope deferred, he said----

----How surely, soundly, deeply, the physical underlies the spiritual. This morning I was up and out at half-past four, as perfect a morning as I ever saw: mists yet huddled in the low spots, the sun coming up over the hill, and all the earth fresh with moisture, sweet with good odours, and musical with early bird-notes.

It is the time of the spring just after the last seeding and before the early haying: a catch-breath in the farmer's year. I have been utilising it in digging a drainage ditch at the lower end of my farm. A spot of marsh grass and blue flags occupies nearly half an acre of good land and I have been planning ever since I bought the place to open a drain from its lower edge to the creek, supplementing it in the field above, if necessary, with submerged tiling. I surveyed it carefully several weeks ago and drew plans and contours of the work as though it were an inter-oceanic canal. I find it a real delight to work out in the earth itself the details of the drawing.

This morning, after hastening with the chores, I took my bag and my spade on my shoulder and set off (in rubber boots) for the ditch. My way lay along the margin of my cornfield in the deep grass. On my right as I walked was the old rail fence full of thrifty young hickory and cherry trees with here and there a clump of blackberry bushes. The trees beyond the fence cut off the sunrise so that I walked in the cool broad shadows. On my left stretched the cornfield of my planting, the young corn well up, very attractive and hopeful, my really frightful scarecrow standing guard on the knoll, a wisp of straw sticking up through a hole in his hat and his crooked thumbs turned down--"No mercy."

"Surely no corn ever before grew like this," I said to myself. "To-morrow I must begin cultivating again."

So I looked up and about me--not to miss anything of the morning--and I drew in a good big breath and I thought the world had never been so open to my senses.

I wonder why it is that the sense of smell is so commonly under-regarded. To me it is the source of some of my greatest pleasures. No one of the senses is more often allied with robustity of physical health. A man who smells acutely may be set down as enjoying that which is normal, plain, wholesome. He does not require seasoning: the ordinary earth is good enough for him. He is likely to be sane--which means sound, healthy--in his outlook upon life.

Of all hours of the day there is none like the early morning for downright good odours--the morning before eating. Fresh from sleep and unclogged with food a man's senses cut like knives. The whole world comes in upon him. A still morning is best, for the mists and the moisture seem to retain the odours which they have distilled through the night. Upon a breezy morning one is likely to get a single predominant odour as of clover when the wind blows across a hay field or of apple blossoms when the wind comes through the orchard, but upon a perfectly still morning, it is wonderful how the odours arrange themselves in upright strata, so that one walking passes through them as from room to room in a marvellous temple of fragrance, (I should have said, I think, if I had not been on my way to dig a ditch, that it was like turning the leaves of some delicate volume of lyrics!)

So it was this morning. As I walked along the margin of my field I was conscious, at first, coming within the shadows of the wood, of the cool, heavy aroma which one associates with the night: as of moist woods and earth mould. The penetrating scent of the night remains long after the sights and sounds of it have disappeared. In sunny spots I had the fragrance of the open cornfield, the aromatic breath of the brown earth, giving curiously the sense of fecundity--a warm, generous odour of daylight and sunshine. Down the field, toward the corner, cutting in sharply, as though a door opened (or a page turned to another lyric), came the cloying, sweet fragrance of wild crab-apple blossoms, almost tropical in their richness, and below that, as I came to my work, the thin acrid smell of the marsh, the place of the rushes and the flags and the frogs.

How few of us really use our senses! I mean give ourselves fully at any time to the occupation of the senses. We do not expect to understand a treatise on Economics without applying our minds to it, nor can we really smell or hear or see or feel without every faculty alert. Through sheer indolence we miss half the joy of the world!

Often as I work I stop to see: really see: see everything, or to listen, and it is the wonder of wonders, how much there is in this old world which we never dreamed of, how many beautiful, curious, interesting sights and sounds there are which ordinarily make no impression upon our clogged, overfed and preoccupied minds. I have also had the feeling--it may be unscientific but it is comforting--that any man might see like an Indian or smell like a hound if he gave to the senses the brains which the Indian and the hound apply to them. And I'm pretty sure about the Indian! It is marvellous what a man can do when he puts his entire mind upon one faculty and bears down hard.

So I walked this morning, not hearing nor seeing, but smelling. Without desiring to stir up strife among the peaceful senses, there is this further marvel of the sense of smell. No other possesses such an after-call. Sight preserves pictures: the complete view of the aspect of objects, but it is photographic and external. Hearing deals in echoes, but the sense of smell, while saving no vision of a place or a person, will re-create in a way almost miraculous the inner *emotion* of a particular time or place. I know of nothing that will so "create an appetite under the ribs of death."

Only a short time ago I passed an open doorway in the town. I was busy with errands, my mind fully engaged, but suddenly I caught an odour from somewhere within the building I was passing. I stopped! It was as if in that moment I lost twenty years of my life: I was a boy again, living and feeling a particular instant at the time of my father's death. Every emotion of that occasion, not recalled in years, returned to me sharply and clearly as though I experienced it for the first time. It was a peculiar emotion: the first time I had ever felt the oppression of space--can I describe it?--the utter bigness of the world and the aloofness of myself, a little boy, within it--now that my father was gone. It was not at that moment sorrow, nor remorse, nor love: it was an inexpressible cold terror--that anywhere I might go in the world, I should still be alone!

And there I stood, a man grown, shaking in the sunshine with that old boyish emotion brought back to me by an odour! Often and often have I known this strange rekindling of dead fires. And I have thought how, if our senses were really perfect, we might lose nothing, out of our lives: neither sights, nor sounds, nor emotions: a sort of mortal immortality. Was not Shakespeare great because he lost less of the savings of his senses than other men? What a wonderful seer, hearer, smeller, taster, feeler, he must have been--and how, all the time, his mind must have played upon the gatherings of his senses! All scenes, all men, the very turn of a head, the exact sound of a voice, the taste of food, the feel of the world--all the emotions of his life must he have had there before him as he wrote, his great mind playing upon them, reconstructing, re-creating and putting them down hot upon his pages. There is nothing strange about great men; they are like us, only deeper, higher, broader: they think as we do, but with more intensity: they suffer as we do, more keenly: they love as we do, more tenderly.

I may be over-glorifying the sense of smell, but it is only because I walked this morning in a world of odours. The greatest of the senses, of course, is not smell or hearing, but sight. What would not any man exchange for that: for the faces one loves, for the scenes one holds most dear, for all that is beautiful and changeable and beyond description? The Scotch Preacher says that the saddest lines in all literature are those of Milton, writing of his blindness.

"Seasons return; but not to me returns Day, or the sweet approach of even or morn, Or sight of vernal bloom or Summer's rose, Or flocks, or herds, or human face divine."

--I have wandered a long way from ditch-digging, but not wholly without intention. Sooner or later I try to get back into the main road. I throw down my spade in the wet trampled grass at the edge of the ditch. I take off my coat and hang it over a limb of the little hawthorn tree. I put my bag near it. I roll up the sleeves of my flannel shirt: I give my hat a twirl; I'm ready for work.

--The senses are the tools by which we lay hold upon the world: they are the implements of consciousness and growth. So long as they are used upon the good earth--used to wholesome weariness--they remain healthy, they yield enjoyment, they nourish growth; but let them once be removed from their natural employment and they turn and feed upon themselves, they seek the stimulation of luxury, they wallow in their own corruption, and finally, worn out, perish from off the earth which they have not appreciated. Vice is ever the senses gone astray.

--So I dug. There is something fine in hard physical labour, straight ahead: no brain used, just muscles. I stood ankle-deep in the cool water: every spadeful came out with a smack, and as I turned it over at the edge of the ditch small turgid rivulets coursed back again. I did not think of anything in particular. I dug. A peculiar joy attends the very pull of the muscles. I drove the spade home with one foot, then I bent and lifted and turned with a sort of physical satisfaction difficult to describe. At first I had the cool of the morning, but by seven o'clock the day was hot enough! I opened the breast of my shirt, gave my sleeves another roll, and went at it again for half an hour, until I dripped with perspiration.

"I will knock off," I said, so I used my spade as a ladder and climbed out of the ditch. Being very thirsty, I walked down through the marshy valley to the clump of alders which grows along the creek. I followed a cow-path through the thicket and came to the creek side, where I knelt on a log and took a good long drink. Then I soused my head in the cool stream, dashed the water upon my arms and came up dripping and gasping! Oh, but it was fine!

So I came back to the hawthorn tree, where I sat down comfortably and stretched my legs. There is a poem in stretched legs--after hard digging--but I can't write it, though I can feel it! I got my bag and took out a half loaf of Harriet's bread. Breaking off big crude pieces, I ate it there in the shade. How rarely we taste the real taste of bread! We disguise it with butter, we toast it, we eat it with milk or fruit. We even soak it with gravy (here in the country where we aren't at all polite--but very comfortable), so that we never get the downright delicious taste of the bread itself. I was hungry this morning and I ate my half loaf to the last crumb--and wanted more. Then I lay down for a moment in the shade and looked up into the sky through the thin outer branches of the hawthorn. A turkey buzzard was lazily circling cloud-high above me: a frog boomed intermittently from the little marsh, and there were bees at work in the blossoms.

--I had another drink at the creek and went back somewhat reluctantly, I confess, to the work. It was hot, and the first joy of effort had worn off. But the ditch was to be dug and I went at it again. One becomes a sort of machine--unthinking, mechanical: and yet intense physical work, though making no immediate impression on the mind, often lingers in the consciousness. I find that sometimes I can remember and enjoy for long afterward every separate step in a task.

It is curious, hard physical labour! One actually stops thinking. I often work long without any thought whatever, so far as I know, save that connected with the monotonous repetition of the labour itself--down with the spade, out with it, up with it, over with it--and repeat. And yet sometimes--mostly in the forenoon when I am not at all tired--I will suddenly have a sense as of the world opening around me--a sense of its beauty and its meanings--giving me a peculiar deep happiness, that is near complete content--

Happiness, I have discovered, is nearly always a rebound from hard work. It is one of the follies of men to imagine that they can enjoy mere thought, or emotion, or sentiment! As well try to eat beauty! For happiness must be tricked! She loves to see men at work. She loves sweat, weariness, self-sacrifice. She will be found not in palaces but lurking in cornfields and factories and hovering over littered desks: she crowns the unconscious head of the busy child. If you look up suddenly from hard work you will see her, but if you look too long she fades sorrowfully away.

--Down toward the town there is a little factory for barrel hoops and staves. It has one of the most musical whistles I ever heard in my life. It toots at exactly twelve o'clock: blessed sound! The last half-hour at ditch-digging is a hard, slow pull. I'm warm and tired, but I stick down to it and wait with straining ear for the music. At the very first note, of that whistle I drop my spade. I will even empty out a load of dirt half way up rather than expend another ounce of energy; and I spring out of the ditch and start for home with a single desire in my heart--or possibly lower down. And Harriet, standing in the doorway, seems to me a sort of angel--a culinary angel!

Talk of joy: there may be things better than beef stew and baked potatoes and home-made bread--there may be--

VII
AN ARGUMENT WITH A MILLIONNAIRE

"Let the mighty and great
  Roll in splendour and state,
  I envy them not, I declare it.
  I eat my own lamb,
  My own chicken and ham,
  I shear my own sheep and wear it.

  I have lawns, I have bowers,
  I have fruits, I have flowers.
  The lark is my morning charmer;
  So you jolly dogs now,
  Here's God bless the plow--
  Long life and content to the farmer."

---- *Rhyme on an old pitcher of English pottery*.

I have been hearing of John Starkweather ever since I came here. He is a most important personage in this community. He is rich. Horace especially loved to talk about him. Give Horace half a chance, whether the subject be pigs or churches, and he will break in somewhere with the remark: "As I was saying to Mr. Starkweather--" or, "Mr. Starkweather says to me--" How we love to shine by reflected glory! Even Harriet has not gone unscathed; she, too, has been affected by the bacillus of admiration. She has wanted to know several times if I saw John Starkweather drive by: "the finest span of horses in this country," she says, and "*did* you see his daughter?" Much other information concerning the Starkweather household, culinary and otherwise, is current among our hills. We know accurately the number of Mr. Starkweather's bedrooms, we can tell how much coal he uses in winter and how many tons of ice in summer, and upon such important premises we argue his riches.

Several times I have passed John Starkweather's home. It lies between my farm and the town, though not on the direct road, and it is really beautiful with the groomed and guided beauty possible to wealth. A stately old house with a huge end chimney of red brick stands with dignity well back from the road; round about lie pleasant lawns that once were cornfields: and there are drives and walks and exotic shrubs. At first, loving my own hills so well, I was puzzled to understand why I should also enjoy Starkweather's groomed surroundings. But it came to me that after all, much as we may love wildness, we are not wild, nor our works. What more artificial than a house, or a barn, or a fence? And the greater and more formal the house, the more formal indeed must be the nearer natural environments. Perhaps the hand of man might well have been less evident in developing the surroundings of the Starkweather home--for art, dealing with nature, is so often too accomplished!

But I enjoy the Starkweather place and as I look in from the road, I sometimes think to myself with satisfaction: "Here is this rich man who has paid his thousands to make the beauty which I pass and take for nothing--and having taken, leave as much behind." And I wonder sometimes whether he, inside his fences, gets more joy of it than I, who walk the roads outside. Anyway, I am grateful to him for using his riches so much to my advantage.

On fine mornings John Starkweather sometimes comes out in his slippers, bareheaded, his white vest gleaming in the sunshine, and walks slowly around his garden. Charles Baxter says that on these occasions he is asking his gardener the names of the vegetables. However that may be, he has seemed to our community the very incarnation of contentment and prosperity--his position the acme of desirability.

What was my astonishment, then, the other morning to see John Starkweather coming down the pasture lane through my farm. I knew him afar off, though I had never met him. May I express the inexpressible when I say he had a rich look; he walked rich, there was richness in the confident crook of his elbow, and in the positive twitch of the stick he carried: a man accustomed to having doors opened before he knocked. I stood there a moment and looked up the hill at him, and I felt that profound curiosity which every one of us feels every day of his life to know something of the inner impulses which stir his nearest neighbour. I should have liked to know John Starkweather; but I thought to myself as I have thought so many times how surely one comes finally to imitate his surroundings. A farmer grows to be a part of his farm; the sawdust on his coat is not the most distinctive insignia of the carpenter; the poet writes his truest lines upon his own countenance. People passing in my road take me to be a part of this natural scene. I suppose I seem to them as a partridge squatting among dry grass and leaves, so like the grass and leaves as to be invisible. We all come to be marked upon by nature and dismissed--how carelessly!--as genera or species. And is it not the primal struggle of man to escape classification, to form new differentiations?

Sometimes--I confess it--when I see one passing in my road, I feel like hailing him and saying:

"Friend, I am not all farmer. I, too, am a person; I am different and curious. I am full of red blood, I like people, all sorts of people; if you are not interested in me, at least I am intensely interested in you. Come over now and let's talk!"

So we are all of us calling and calling across the incalculable gulfs which separate us even from our nearest friends!

Once or twice this feeling has been so real to me that I've been near to the point of hailing utter strangers--only to be instantly overcome with a sense of the humorous absurdity of such an enterprise. So I laugh it off and I say to myself:

"Steady now: the man is going to town to sell a pig; he is coming back with ten pounds of sugar, five of salt pork, a can of coffee and some new blades for his mowing machine. He hasn't time for talk"--and so I come down with a bump to my digging, or hoeing, or chopping, or whatever it is.

----Here I've left John Starkweather in my pasture while I remark to the extent of a page or two that I didn't expect him to see me when he went by.

I assumed that he was out for a walk, perhaps to enliven a worn appetite (do you know, confidentially, I've had some pleasure in times past in reflecting upon the jaded appetites of millionnaires!), and that he would pass out by my lane to the country road; but instead of that, what should he do but climb the yard fence and walk over toward the barn where I was at work.

Perhaps I was not consumed with excitement: here was fresh adventure!

"A farmer," I said to myself with exultation, "has only to wait long enough and all the world comes his way."

I had just begun to grease my farm wagon and was experiencing some difficulty in lifting and steadying the heavy rear axle while I took off the wheel. I kept busily at work, pretending (such is the perversity of the human mind) that I did not see Mr. Starkweather. He stood for a moment watching me; then he said:

"Good morning, sir."

I looked up and said:

"Oh, good morning!"

"Nice little farm you have here."

"It's enough for me," I replied. I did not especially like the "little." One is human.

Then I had an absurd inspiration: he stood there so trim and jaunty and prosperous. So rich! I had a good look at him. He was dressed in a woollen jacket coat, knee-trousers and leggins; on his head he wore a jaunty, cocky little Scotch cap; a man, I should judge, about fifty years old, well-fed and hearty in appearance, with grayish hair and a good-humoured eye. I acted on my inspiration:

"You've arrived," I said, "at the psychological moment."

"How's that?"

"Take hold here and help me lift this axle and steady it. I'm having a hard time of it."

The look of astonishment in his countenance was beautiful to see.

For a moment failure stared me in the face. His expression said with emphasis: "Perhaps you don't know who I am." But I looked at him with the greatest good feeling and my expression said, or I meant it to say: "To be sure I don't: and what difference does it make, anyway!"

"You take hold there," I said, without waiting for him to catch his breath, "and I'll get hold here. Together we can easily get the wheel off."

Without a word he set his cane against the barn and bent his back, up came the axle and I propped it with a board.

"Now," I said, "you hang on there and steady it while I get the wheel off"-- though, indeed, it didn't really need much steadying.

As I straightened up, whom should I see but Harriet standing transfixed in the pathway half way down to the barn, transfixed with horror. She had recognised John Starkweather and had heard at least part of what I said to him, and the vision of that important man bending his back to help lift the axle of my old wagon was too terrible! She caught my eye and pointed and mouthed. When I smiled and nodded, John Starkweather straightened up and looked around.

"Don't, on your life," I warned, "let go of that axle."

He held on and Harriet turned and retreated ingloriously. John Starkweather's face was a study!

"Did you ever grease a wagon?" I asked him genially.

"Never," he said.

"There's more of an art in it than you think," I said, and as I worked I talked to him of the lore of axle-grease and showed him exactly how to put it on--neither too much nor too little, and so that it would distribute itself evenly when the wheel was replaced.

"There's a right way of doing everything," I observed.

"That's so," said John Starkweather: "if I could only get workmen that believed it."

By that time I could see that he was beginning to be interested. I put back the wheel, gave it a light turn and screwed on the nut. He helped me with the other end of the axle with all good humour.

"Perhaps," I said, as engagingly as I knew how, "you'd like to try the art yourself? You take the grease this time and I'll steady the wagon."

"All right!" he said, laughing, "I'm in for anything."

He took the grease box and the paddle--less gingerly than I thought he would.

"Is that right?" he demanded, and so he put on the grease. And oh, it was good to see Harriet in the doorway!

"Steady there," I said, "not so much at the end: now put the box down on the reach."

And so together we greased the wagon, talking all the time in the friendliest way. I actually believe that he was having a pretty good time. At least it had the virtue of unexpectedness. He wasn't bored!

When he had finished we both straightened our backs and looked at each other. There was a twinkle in his eye: then we both laughed. "He's all right," I said to myself. I held up my hands, then he held up his: it was hardly necessary to prove that wagon-greasing was not a delicate operation.

"It's a good wholesome sign," I said, "but it'll come off. Do you happen to remember a story of Tolstoi's called Ivan the Fool'?"

("What is a farmer doing quoting Tolstoi!" remarked his countenance--though he said not a word.)

"In the kingdom of Ivan, you remember," I said, "it was the rule that whoever had hard places on his hands came to table, but whoever had not must eat what the others left."

Thus I led him up to the back steps and poured him a basin of hot water--which I brought myself from the kitchen, Harriet having marvellously and completely disappeared. We both washed our hands, talking with great good humour.

When we had finished I said:

"Sit down, friend, if you've time, and let's talk."

So he sat down on one of the logs of my woodpile: a solid sort of man, rather warm after his recent activities. He looked me over with some interest and, I thought, friendliness.

"Why does a man like you," he asked finally, "waste himself on a little farm back here in the country?"

For a single instant I came nearer to being angry than I have been for a long time. **Waste** myself! So we are judged without knowledge. I had a sudden impulse to demolish him (if I could) with the nearest sarcasms I could lay hand to. He was so sure of himself! "Oh well," I thought, with vainglorious superiority, "he doesn't know," So I said:

"What would you have me be--a millionnaire?"

He smiled, but with a sort of sincerity.

"You might be," he said: "who can tell!"

I laughed outright: the humour of it struck me as delicious. Here I had been, ever since I first heard of John Starkweather, rather gloating over him as a poor suffering millionnaire (of course millionnaires *are* unhappy), and there he sat, ruddy of face and hearty of body, pitying *me* for a poor unfortunate farmer back here in the country! Curious, this human nature of ours, isn't it? But how infinitely beguiling!

So I sat down beside Mr. Starkweather on the log and crossed my legs. I felt as though I had set foot in a new country.

"Would you really advise me," I asked, "to start in to be a millionnaire?"

He chuckled:

"Well, that's one way of putting it. Hitch your wagon to a star; but begin by making a few dollars more a year than you spend. When I began----" he stopped short with an amused smile, remembering that I did not know who he was.

"Of course," I said, "I understand that."

"A man must begin small"--he was on pleasant ground--"and anywhere he likes, a few dollars here, a few there. He must work hard, he must save, he must be both bold and cautious. I know a man who began when he was about your age with total assets of ten dollars and a good digestion. He's now considered a fairly wealthy man. He has a home in the city, a place in the country, and he goes to Europe when he likes. He has so arranged his affairs that young men do most of the work and he draws the dividends--and all in a little more than twenty years. I made every single cent--but as I said, it's a penny business to start with. The point is, I like to see young men ambitious."

"Ambitious," I asked, "for what?"

"Why, to rise in the world; to get ahead."

"I know you'll pardon me," I said, "for appearing to cross-examine you, but I'm tremendously interested in these things. What do you mean by rising? And who am I to get ahead of?"

He looked at me in astonishment, and with evident impatience at my consummate stupidity.

"I am serious," I said. "I really want to make the best I can of my life. It's the only one I've got."

"See here," he said: "let us say you clear up five hundred a year from this farm----"

"You exaggerate--" I interrupted.

"Do I?" he laughed; "that makes my case all the better. Now, isn't it possible to rise from that? Couldn't you make a thousand or five thousand or even fifty thousand a year?"

It seems an unanswerable argument: fifty thousand dollars!

"I suppose I might," I said, "but do you think I'd be any better off or happier with fifty thousand a year than I am now? You see, I like all these surroundings better than any other place I ever knew. That old green hill over there with the oak on it is an intimate friend of mine. I have a good cornfield in which every year I work miracles. I've a cow and a horse, and a few pigs. I have a comfortable home. My appetite is perfect, and I have plenty of food to gratify it. I sleep every night like a boy, for I haven't a trouble in this world to disturb me. I enjoy the mornings here in the country: and the evenings are pleasant. Some of my neighbours have come to be my good friends. I like them and I am pretty sure they like me. Inside the house there I have the best books ever written and I have time in the evenings to read them--I mean *really* read them. Now the question is, would I be any better off, or any happier, if I had fifty thousand a year?"

John Starkweather laughed.

"Well, sir," he said, "I see I've made the acquaintance of a philosopher."

"Let us say," I continued, "that you are willing to invest twenty years of your life in a million dollars." ("Merely an illustration," said John Starkweather.) "You have it where you can put it in the bank and take it out again, or you can give it form in houses, yachts, and other things. Now twenty years of my life--to me--is worth more than a million dollars. I simply can't afford to sell it for that. I prefer to invest it, as somebody or other has said, unearned in life. I've always had a liking for intangible properties."

"See here," said John Starkweather, "you are taking a narrow view of life. You are making your own pleasure the only standard. Shouldn't a man make the most of the talents given him? Hasn't he a duty to society?"

"Now you are shifting your ground," I said, "from the question of personal satisfaction to that of duty. That concerns me, too. Let me ask you: Isn't it important to society that this piece of earth be plowed and cultivated?"

"Yes, but----"

"Isn't it honest and useful work?"

"Of course."

"Isn't it important that it shall not only be done, but well done?"

"Certainly."

"It takes all there is in a good man," I said, "to be a good farmer."

"But the point is," he argued, "might not the same faculties applied to other things yield better and bigger results?"

"That is a problem, of course," I said. "I tried money-making once--in a city--and I was unsuccessful and unhappy; here I am both successful and happy. I suppose I was one of the young men who did the work while some millionnaire drew the dividends." (I was cutting close, and I didn't venture to look at him). "No doubt he had his houses and yachts and went to Europe when he liked. I know I lived upstairs--back--where there wasn't a tree to be seen, or a spear of green grass, or a hill, or a brook: only smoke and chimneys and littered roofs. Lord be thanked for my escape! Sometimes I think that Success has formed a silent conspiracy against Youth. Success holds up a single glittering apple and bids Youth strip and run for it; and Youth runs and Success still holds the apple."

John Starkweather said nothing.

"Yes," I said, "there are duties. We realise, we farmers, that we must produce more than we ourselves can eat or wear or burn. We realise that we are the foundation: we connect human life with the earth. We dig and plant and produce, and having eaten at the first table ourselves, we pass what is left to the bankers and millionnaires. Did you ever think, stranger, that most of the wars of the world have been fought for the control of this farmer's second table? Have you thought that the surplus of wheat and corn and cotton is what the railroads are struggling to carry? Upon our surplus run all the factories and mills; a little of it gathered in cash makes a millionnaire. But we farmers, we sit back comfortably after dinner, and joke with our wives and play with our babies, and let all the rest of you fight for the crumbs that fall from our abundant tables. If once we really cared and got up and shook ourselves, and said to the maid: 'Here, child, don't waste the crusts: gather 'em up and to-morrow we'll have a cottage pudding,' where in the world would all the millionnaires be?"

Oh, I tell you, I waxed eloquent. I couldn't let John Starkweather, or any other man, get away with the conviction that a millionnaire is better than a farmer. "Moreover," I said, "think of the position of the millionnaire. He spends his time playing not with life, but with the symbols of life, whether cash or houses. Any day the symbols may change; a little war may happen along, there may be a defective flue or a western breeze, or even a panic because the farmers aren't scattering as many crumbs as usual (they call it crop failure, but I've noticed that the farmers still continue to have plenty to eat) and then what happens to your millionnaire? Not knowing how to produce anything himself, he would starve to death if there were not always, somewhere, a farmer to take him up to the table."

"You're making a strong case," laughed John Starkweather.

"Strong!" I said. "It is simply wonderful what a leverage upon society a few acres of land, a cow, a pig or two, and a span of horses gives a man. I'm ridiculously independent. I'd be the hardest sort of a man to dislodge or crush. I tell you, my friend, a farmer is like an oak, his roots strike deep in the soil, he draws a sufficiency of food from the earth itself, he breathes the free air around him, his thirst is quenched by heaven itself--and there's no tax on sunshine."

I paused for very lack of breath. John Starkweather was laughing.

"When you commiserate me, therefore" ("I'm sure I shall never do it again," said John Starkweather)--"when you commiserate me, therefore, and advise me to rise, you must give me really good reasons for changing my occupation and becoming a millionnaire. You must prove to me that I can be more independent, more honest, more useful as a millionnaire, and that I shall have better and truer friends!"

John Starkweather looked around at me (I knew I had been absurdly eager and I was rather ashamed of myself) and put his hand on my knee (he has a wonderfully fine eye!).

"I don't believe," he said, "you'd have any truer friends."

"Anyway," I said repentantly, "I'll admit that millionnaires have their place-- at present I wouldn't do entirely away with them, though I do think they'd enjoy farming better. And if I were to select a millionnaire for all the best things I know, I should certainly choose you, Mr. Starkweather."

He jumped up.

"You know who I am?" he asked.

I nodded.

"And you knew all the time?"

I nodded.

"Well, you're a good one!"

We both laughed and fell to talking with the greatest friendliness. I led him down my garden to show him my prize pie-plant, of which I am enormously proud, and I pulled for him some of the finest stalks I could find.

"Take it home," I said, "it makes the best pies of any pie-plant in this country."

He took it under his arm.

"I want you to come over and see me the first chance you get," he said. "I'm going to prove to you by physical demonstration that it's better sport to be a millionnaire than a farmer--not that I am a millionnaire: I'm only accepting the reputation you give me."

So I walked with him down to the lane.

"Let me know when you grease up again," he said, "and I'll come over."

So we shook hands: and he set off sturdily down the road with the pie-plant leaves waving cheerfully over his shoulder.

VIII
A BOY AND A PREACHER

This morning I went to church with Harriet. I usually have some excuse for not going, but this morning I had them out one by one and they were altogether so shabby that I decided not to use them. So I put on my stiff shirt and Harriet came out in her best black cape with the silk fringes. She looked so immaculate, so ruddy, so cheerfully sober (for Sunday) that I was reconciled to the idea of driving her up to the church. And I am glad I went, for the experience I had.

It was an ideal summer Sunday: sunshiny, clear and still. I believe if I had been some Rip Van Winkle waking after twenty years' sleep I should have known it for Sunday. Away off over the hill somewhere we could hear a lazy farm boy singing at the top of his voice: the higher cadences of his song reached us pleasantly through the still air. The hens sitting near the lane fence, fluffing the dust over their backs, were holding a small and talkative service of their own. As we turned into the main road we saw the Patterson children on their way to church, all the little girls in Sunday ribbons, and all the little boys very uncomfortable in knit stockings.

"It seems a pity to go to church on a day like this," I said to Harriet.

"A pity!" she exclaimed. "Could anything be more appropriate?"

Harriet is good because she can't help it. Poor woman!--but I haven't any pity for her.

It sometimes seems to me the more worshipful I feel the less I want to go to church. I don't know why it is, but these forms, simple though they are, trouble me. The moment an emotion, especially a religious emotion, becomes an institution, it somehow loses life. True emotion is rare and costly and that which is awakened from without never rises to the height of that which springs spontaneously from within.

Back of the church stands a long low shed where we tied our horse. A number of other buggies were already there, several women were standing in groups, preening their feathers, a neighbour of ours who has a tremendous bass voice was talking to a friend:

"Yas, oats is showing up well, but wheat is backward."

His voice, which he was evidently trying to subdue for Sunday, boomed through the still air. So we walked among the trees to the door of the church. A smiling elder, in an unaccustomed long coat, bowed and greeted us. As we went in there was an odour of cushions and our footsteps on the wooden floor echoed in the warm emptiness of the church. The Scotch preacher was finding his place in the big Bible; he stood solid and shaggy behind the yellow oak pulpit, a peculiar professional look on his face. In the pulpit the Scotch preacher is too much minister, too little man. He is best down among us with his hand in ours. He is a sort of human solvent. Is there a twisted and hardened heart in the community he beams upon it from his cheerful eye, he speaks out of his great charity, he gives the friendly pressure of his large hand, and that hardened heart dissolves and its frozen hopelessness loses itself in tears. So he goes through life, seeming always to understand. He is not surprised by wickedness nor discouraged by weakness: he is so sure of a greater Strength!

But I must come to my experience, which I am almost tempted to call a resurrection--the resurrection of a boy, long since gone away, and of a tall lank preacher who, in his humility, looked upon himself as a failure. I hardly know how it all came back to me; possibly it was the scent-laden breeze that came in from the woods and through the half-open church window, perhaps it was a line in one of the old songs, perhaps it was the droning voice of the Scotch preacher--somehow, and suddenly, I was a boy again.

----To this day I think of death as a valley: a dark shadowy valley: the Valley of the Shadow of Death. So persistent are the impressions of boyhood! As I sat in the church I could see, as distinctly as though I were there, the church of my boyhood and the tall dyspeptic preacher looming above the pulpit, the peculiar way the light came through the coarse colour of the windows, the barrenness and stiffness of the great empty room, the raw girders overhead, the prim choir. There was something in that preacher, gaunt, worn, sodden though he appeared: a spark somewhere, a little flame, mostly smothered by the gray dreariness of his surroundings, and yet blazing up at times to some warmth.

As I remember it, our church was a church of failures. They sent us the old gray preachers worn out in other fields. Such a succession of them I remember, each with some peculiarity, some pathos. They were of the old sort, indoctrinated Presbyterians, and they harrowed well our barren field with the tooth of their hard creed. Some thundered the Law, some pleaded Love; but of all of them I remember best the one who thought himself the greatest failure. I think he had tried a hundred churches--a hard life, poorly paid, unappreciated--in a new country. He had once had a family, but one by one they had died. No two were buried in the same cemetery; and finally, before he came to our village, his wife, too, had gone. And he was old, and out of health, and discouraged: seeking some final warmth from his own cold doctrine. How I see him, a trifle bent, in his long worn coat, walking in the country roads: not knowing of a boy who loved him!

He told my father once: I recall his exact, words:

"My days have been long, and I have failed. It was not given me to reach men's hearts."

Oh, gray preacher, may I now make amends? Will you forgive me? I was a boy and did not know; a boy whose emotions were hidden under mountains of reserve: who could have stood up to be shot more easily than he could have said: "I love you!"

Of that preacher's sermons I remember not one word, though I must have heard scores of them--only that they were interminably long and dull and that my legs grew weary of sitting and that I was often hungry. It was no doubt the dreadful old doctrine that he preached, thundering the horrors of disobedience, urging an impossible love through fear and a vain belief without reason. All that touched me not at all, save with a sort of wonder at the working of his great Adam's apple and the strange rollings of his cavernous eyes. This he looked upon as the work of God; thus for years he had sought, with self-confessed failure, to touch the souls of his people. How we travel in darkness and the work we do in all seriousness counts for naught, and the thing we toss off in play-time, unconsciously, God uses!

One tow-headed boy sitting there in a front row dreaming dreams, if the sermons touched him not, was yet thrilled to the depths of his being by that tall preacher. Somewhere, I said, he had a spark within him. I think he never knew it: or if he knew it, he regarded it as a wayward impulse that might lead him from his God. It was a spark of poetry: strange flower in such a husk. In times of emotion it bloomed, but in daily life it emitted no fragrance. I have wondered what might have been if some one--some understanding woman--had recognised his gift, or if he himself as a boy had once dared to cut free! We do not know: we do not know the tragedy of our nearest friend!

By some instinct the preacher chose his readings mostly from the Old Testament--those splendid, marching passages, full of oriental imagery. As he read there would creep into his voice a certain resonance that lifted him and his calling suddenly above his gray surroundings.

How vividly I recall his reading of the twenty-third Psalm--a particular reading. I suppose I had heard the passage many times before, but upon this certain morning----

Shall I ever forget? The windows were open, for it was May, and a boy could look out on the hillside and see with longing eyes the inviting grass and trees. A soft wind blew in across the church; it was full of the very essence of spring. I smell it yet. On the pulpit stood a bunch of crocuses crowded into a vase: some Mary's offering. An old man named Johnson who sat near us was already beginning to breathe heavily, preparatory to sinking into his regular Sunday snore. Then those words from the preacher, bringing me suddenly--how shall I express it?--out of some formless void, to intense consciousness--a miracle of creation:

"Yea though I walk through the valley of the shadow of death, I will fear no evil: for thou art with me; thy rod and thy staff they comfort me."

Well, I saw the way to the place of death that morning; far more vividly I saw it than any natural scene I know: and myself walking therein. I shall know it again when I come to pass that way; the tall, dark, rocky cliffs, the shadowy path within, the overhanging dark branches, even the whitened dead bones by the way--and as one of the vivid phantasms of boyhood--cloaked figures I saw, lurking mysteriously in deep recesses, fearsome for their very silence. And yet I with magic rod and staff walking within--boldly, fearing no evil, full of faith, hope, courage, love, invoking images of terror but for the joy of braving them. Ah, tow-headed boy, shall I tread as lightly that dread pathway when I come to it? Shall I, like you, fear no evil!

So that great morning went away. I heard nothing of singing or sermon and came not to myself until my mother, touching my arm, asked me if I had been asleep! And I smiled and thought how little grown people knew--and I looked up at the sad sick face of the old preacher with a new interest and friendliness. I felt, somehow, that he too was a familiar of my secret valley. I should have liked to ask him, but I did not dare. So I followed my mother when she went to speak to him, and when he did not see, I touched his coat.

After that how I watched when he came to the reading. And one great Sunday, he chose a chapter from Ecclesiastes, the one that begins sonorously:

"Remember now thy creator in the days of thy youth."

Surely that gaunt preacher had the true fire in his gray soul. How his voice dwelt and quivered and softened upon the words!

"While the sun, or the light, or the moon, or the stars, be not darkened, nor the clouds return after the rain----" Thus he brought in the universe to that small church and filled the heart of a boy.

"In the days when the keepers of the house shall tremble, and the strong men shall bow themselves, and the grinders cease because they are few, and those that look out of the windows be darkened."

"And the doors shall be shut in the streets, when the sound of the grinding is low, and he shall rise up at the voice of the bird and all the daughters of music shall be brought low."

Do not think that I understood the meaning of those passages: I am not vain enough to think I know even now--but the *sound* of them, the roll of them, the beautiful words, and above all, the pictures!

Those Daughters of Music, how I lived for days imagining them! They were of the trees and the hills, and they were very beautiful but elusive; one saw them as he heard singing afar off, sweet strains fading often into silences. Daughters of Music! Daughters of Music! And why should they be brought low?

Doors shut in the street--how I *saw* them--a long, long street, silent, full of sunshine, and the doors shut, and no sound anywhere but the low sound of the grinding: and the mill with the wheels drowsily turning and no one there at all save one boy with fluttering heart, tiptoeing in the sunlit doorway.

And the voice of the bird. Not the song but the *voice*. Yes, a bird had a voice.

I had known it always, and yet somehow I had not dared to say it. I felt that they would look at me with that questioning, incredulous look which I dreaded beyond belief. They might laugh! But here it was in the Book--the voice of a bird. How my appreciation of that Book increased and what a new confidence it gave me in my own images! I went about for days, listening, listening, listening--and interpreting.

So the words of the preacher and the fire in them:

"And when they shall be afraid of that which is high and fears shall be in the way----"

I knew the fear of that which is high: I had dreamed of it commonly. And I knew also the Fear that stood in the way: him I had seen in a myriad of forms, looming black by darkness in every lane I trod; and yet with what defiance I met and slew him!

And then, more thrilling than all else, the words of the preacher:

"Or ever the silver cord be loosed, or the golden bowl be broken, or the pitcher be broken at the fountain, or the wheel broken at the cistern."

Such pictures: that silver cord, that golden bowl! And why and wherefore?

A thousand ways I turned them in my mind--and always with the sound of the preacher's voice in my ears--the resonance of the words conveying an indescribable fire of inspiration. Vaguely and yet with certainty I knew the preacher spoke out of some unfathomable emotion which I did not understand--which I did not care to understand. Since then I have thought what those words must have meant to him!

Ah, that tall lank preacher, who thought himself a failure: how long I shall remember him and the words he read and the mournful yet resonant cadences of his voice--and the barren church, and the stony religion! Heaven he gave me, unknowing, while he preached an ineffectual hell.

As we rode home Harriet looked into my face.

"You have enjoyed the service," she said softly.

"Yes," I said.

"It *was* a good sermon," she said.

"Was it?" I replied.

IX
THE TRAMP

I have had a new and strange experience--droll in one way, grotesque in another and when everything is said, tragic: at least an adventure. Harriet looks at me accusingly, and I have had to preserve the air of one deeply contrite now for two days (no easy accomplishment for me!), even though in secret I have smiled and pondered.

How our life has been warped by books! We are not contented with realities: we crave conclusions. With what ardour our minds respond to real events with literary deductions. Upon a train of incidents, as unconnected as life itself, we are wont to clap a booky ending. An instinctive desire for completeness animates the human mind (a struggle to circumscribe the infinite). We would like to have life "turn out"--but it doesn't--it doesn't. Each event is the beginning of a whole new genealogy of events. In boyhood I remember asking after every story I heard: "What happened next?" for no conclusion ever quite satisfied me--even when the hero died in his own gore. I always knew there was something yet remaining to be told. The only sure conclusion we can reach is this: Life changes. And what is more enthralling to the human mind than this splendid, boundless, coloured mutability!--life in the making? How strange it is, then, that we should be contented to take such small parts of it as we can grasp, and to say, "This is the true explanation." By such devices we seek to bring infinite existence within our finite egoistic grasp. We solidify and define where solidification means loss of interest; and loss of interest, not years, is old age.

So I have mused since my tramp came in for a moment out of the Mystery (as we all do) and went away again into the Mystery (in our way, too).

There are strange things in this world!

*   *   *   *   *

As I came around the corner I saw sitting there on my steps the very personification of Ruin, a tumble-down, dilapidated wreck of manhood. He gave one the impression of having been dropped where he sat, all in a heap. My first instinctive feeling was not one of recoil or even of hostility, but rather a sudden desire to pick him up and put him where he belonged, the instinct, I should say, of the normal man who hangs his axe always on the same nail. When he saw me he gathered himself together with reluctance and stood fully revealed. It was a curious attitude of mingled effrontery and apology. "Hit me if you dare," blustered his outward personality. "For God's sake, don't hit me," cried the innate fear in his eyes. I stopped and looked at him sharply, His eyes dropped, his look slid away, so that I experienced a sense of shame, as though I had trampled upon him. A damp rag of humanity! I confess that my first impulse, and a strong one, was to kick him for the good of the human race. No man has a right to be like that.

And then, quite suddenly, I had a great revulsion of feeling. What was I that I should judge without knowledge? Perhaps, after all, here was one bearing treasure. So I said:

"You are the man I have been expecting."

He did not reply, only flashed his eyes up at me, wherein fear deepened.

"I have been saving up a coat for you," I said, "and a pair of shoes. They are not much worn," I said, "but a little too small for me. I think they will fit you."

He looked at me again, not sharply, but with a sort of weak cunning. So far he had not said a word.

"I think our supper is nearly ready," I said: "let us go in."

"No, mister," he mumbled, "a bite out here--no, mister"--and then, as though the sound of his own voice inspired him, he grew declamatory.

"I'm a respectable man, mister, plumber by trade, but----"

"But," I interrupted, "you can't get any work, you're cold and you haven't had anything to eat for two days, so you are walking out here in the country where we farmers have no plumbing to do. At home you have a starving wife and three small children----"

"Six, mister----"

"Well, six--And now we will go in to supper."

I led him into the entry way and poured for him a big basin of hot water. As I stepped out again with a comb he was slinking toward the doorway.

"Here," I said, "is a comb; we are having supper now in a few minutes."

I wish I could picture Harriet's face when I brought him into her immaculate kitchen. But I gave her a look, one of the commanding sort that I can put on in times of great emergency, and she silently laid another place at the table.

When I came to look at our Ruin by the full lamplight I was surprised to see what a change a little warm water and a comb had wrought in him. He came to the table uncertain, blinking, apologetic. His forehead, I saw, was really impressive--high, narrow and thin-skinned. His face gave one somehow the impression of a carving once full of significant lines, now blurred and worn as though Time, having first marked it with the lines of character, had grown discouraged and brushed the hand of forgetfulness over her work. He had peculiar thin, silky hair of no particular colour, with a certain almost childish pathetic waviness around the ears and at the back of the neck. Something, after all, about the man aroused one's compassion.

I don't know that he looked dissipated, and surely he was not as dirty as I had at first supposed. Something remained that suggested a care for himself in the past. It was not dissipation, I decided; it was rather an indefinable looseness and weakness, that gave one alternately the feeling I had first experienced, that of anger, succeeded by the compassion that one feels for a child. To Harriet, when she had once seen him, he was all child, and she all compassion.

We disturbed him with no questions. Harriet's fundamental quality is homeliness, comfortableness. Her tea-kettle seems always singing; an indefinable tabbiness, as of feather cushions, lurks in her dining-room, a right warmth of table and chairs, indescribably comfortable at the end of a chilly day. A busy good-smelling steam arises from all her dishes at once, and the light in the middle of the table is of a redness that enthralls the human soul. As for Harriet herself, she is the personification of comfort, airy, clean, warm, inexpressibly wholesome. And never in the world is she so engaging as when she ministers to a man's hunger. Truthfully, sometimes, when she comes to me out of the dimmer light of the kitchen to the radiance of the table with a plate of muffins, it is as though she and the muffins were a part of each other, and that she is really offering some of herself. And down in my heart I know she is doing just that!

Well, it was wonderful to see our Ruin expand in the warmth of Harriet's presence. He had been doubtful of me; of Harriet, I could see, he was absolutely sure. And how he did eat, saying nothing at all, while Harriet plied him with food and talked to me of the most disarming commonplaces. I think it did her heart good to see the way he ate: as though he had had nothing before in days. As he buttered his muffin, not without some refinement, I could see that his hand was long, a curious, lean, ineffectual hand, with a curving little finger. With the drinking of the hot coffee colour began to steal up into his face, and when Harriet brought out a quarter of pie saved over from our dinner and placed it before him--a fine brown pie with small hieroglyphics in the top from whence rose sugary bubbles--he seemed almost to escape himself. And Harriet fairly purred with hospitality.

The more he ate the more of a man he became. His manners improved, his back straightened up, he acquired a not unimpressive poise of the head. Such is the miraculous power of hot muffins and pie!

"As you came down," I asked finally, "did you happen to see old man Masterson's threshing machine?"

"A big red one, with a yellow blow-off?"

"That's the one," I said.

"Well, it was just turning into a field about two miles above here," he replied.

"Big gray, banked barn?" I asked.

"Yes, and a little unpainted house," said our friend.

"That's Parsons'," put in Harriet, with a mellow laugh. "I wonder if he ever *will* paint that house. He builds bigger barns every year and doesn't touch the house. Poor Mrs. Parsons----"

And so we talked of barns and threshing machines in the way we farmers love to do and I lured our friend slowly into talking about himself. At first he was non-committal enough and what he said seemed curiously made to order; he used certain set phrases with which to explain simply what was not easy to explain--a device not uncommon to all of us. I was fearful of not getting within this outward armouring, but gradually as we talked and Harriet poured him a third cup of hot coffee he dropped into a more familiar tone. He told with some sprightliness of having seen threshings in Mexico, how the grain was beaten out with flails in the patios, and afterwards thrown up in the wind to winnow out.

"You must have seen a good deal of life," remarked Harriet sympathetically.

At this remark I saw one of our Ruin's long hands draw up and clinch. He turned his head toward Harriet. His face was partly in the shadow, but there was something striking and strange in the way he looked at her, and a deepness in his voice when he spoke:

"Too much! I've seen too much of life." He threw out one arm and brought it back with a shudder.

"You see what it has left me," he said, "I am an example of too much life."

In response to Harriet's melting compassion he had spoken with unfathomable bitterness. Suddenly he leaned forward toward me with a piercing gaze as though he would look into my soul. His face had changed completely; from the loose and vacant mask of the early evening it had taken on the utmost tensity of emotion.

"You do not know," he said, "what it is to live too much--and to be afraid."

"Live too much?" I asked.

"Yes, live too much, that is what I do--and I am afraid."

He paused a moment and then broke out in a higher key:

"You think I am a tramp. Yes--you do. I know--a worthless fellow, lying, begging, stealing when he can't beg. You have taken me in and fed me. You have said the first kind words I have heard, it seems to me, in years. I don't know who you are. I shall never see you again."

I cannot well describe the intensity of the passion with which he spoke, his face shaking with emotion, his hands trembling.

"Oh, yes," I said easily, "we are comfortable people here--and it is a good place to live."

"No no," he returned. "I know, I've got my call--" Then leaning forward he said in a lower, even more intense voice--"I live everything beforehand."

I was startled by the look of his eyes: the abject terror of it: and I thought to myself, "The man is not right in his mind." And yet I longed to know of the life within this strange husk of manhood.

"I know," he said, as if reading my thought, "you think"--and he tapped his forehead with one finger--"but I'm not. I'm as sane as you are."

It was a strange story he told. It seems almost unbelievable to me as I set it down here, until I reflect how little any one of us knows of the deep life within his nearest neighbour--what stories there are, what tragedies enacted under a calm exterior! What a drama there *may* be in this commonplace man buying ten pounds of sugar at the grocery store, or this other one driving his two old horses in the town road! We do not know. And how rarely are the men of inner adventure articulate! Therefore I treasure the curious story the tramp told me. I do not question its truth. It came as all truth does, through a clouded and unclean medium: and any judgment of the story itself must be based upon a knowledge of the personal equation of the Ruin who told it.

"I am no tramp," he said, "in reality, I am no tramp. I began as well as anyone--It doesn't matter now, only I won't have any of the sympathy that people give to the man who has seen better days. I hate sentiment. *I hate it*----"

I cannot attempt to set down the story in his own words. It was broken with exclamations and involved with wandering sophistries and diatribes of self-blame. His mind had trampled upon itself in throes of introspection until it was often difficult to say which way the paths of the narrative really led. He had thought so much and acted so little that he travelled in a veritable bog of indecision. And yet, withal, some ideas, by constant attrition, had acquired a really striking form. "I am afraid before life," he said. "It makes me dizzy with thought."

At another time he said, "If I am a tramp at all, I am a mental tramp. I have an unanchored mind."

It seems that he came to a realisation that there was something peculiar about him at a very early age. He said they would look at him and whisper to one another and that his sayings were much repeated, often in his hearing. He knew that he was considered an extraordinary child: they baited him with questions that they might laugh at his quaint replies. He said that as early as he could remember he used to plan situations so that he might say things that were strange and even shocking in a child. His father was a small professor in a small college--a "worm" he called him bitterly--"one of those worms that bores in books and finally dries up and blows off." But his mother--he said she was an angel. I recall his exact expression about her eyes that "when she looked at one it made him better." He spoke of her with a softening of the voice, looking often at Harriet. He talked a good deal about his mother, trying to account for himself through her. She was not strong, he said, and very sensitive to the contact of either friends or enemies--evidently a nervous, high-strung woman.

"You have known such people," he said, "everything hurt her."

He said she "starved to death." She starved for affection and understanding.

One of the first things he recalled of his boyhood was his passionate love for his mother.

"I can remember," he said, "lying awake in my bed and thinking how I would love her and serve her--and I could see myself in all sorts of impossible places saving her from danger. When she came to my room to bid me good night, I imagined how I should look--for I have always been able to see myself doing things--when I threw my arms around her neck to kiss her."

Here he reached a strange part of his story. I had been watching Harriet out of the corner of my eye. At first her face was tearful with compassion, but as the Ruin proceeded it became a study in wonder and finally in outright alarm. He said that when his mother came in to bid him good night he saw himself so plainly beforehand ("more vividly than I see you at this moment") and felt his emotion so keenly that when his mother actually stooped to kiss him, somehow he could not respond, he could not throw his arms around her neck. He said he often lay quiet, in waiting, trembling all over until she had gone, not only suffering himself but pitying her, because he understood how she must feel. Then he would follow her, he said, in imagination through the long hall, seeing himself stealing behind her, just touching her hand, wistfully hoping that she might turn to him again--and yet fearing. He said no one knew the agonies he suffered at seeing his mother's disappointment over his apparent coldness and unresponsiveness.

"I think," he said, "it hastened her death." He would not go to the funeral; he did not dare, he said. He cried and fought when they came to take him away, and when the house was silent he ran up to her room and buried his head in her pillows and ran in swift imagination to her funeral. He said he could see himself in the country road, hurrying in the cold rain--for it seemed raining--he said he could actually feel the stones and ruts, although he could not tell how it was possible that he should have seen himself at a distance and *felt* in his own feet the stones of the road. He said he saw the box taken from the wagon-- *saw* it--and that he heard the sound of the clods thrown in, and it made him shriek until they came running and held him.

As he grew older he said he came to live everything beforehand, and that the event as imagined was so far more vivid and affecting that he had no heart for the reality itself.

"It seems strange to you," he said, "but I am telling you exactly what my experience was."

It was curious, he said, when his father told him he must not do a thing, how he went on and imagined in how many different ways he could do it--and how, afterward, he imagined he was punished by that "worm," his father, whom he seemed to hate bitterly. Of those early days, in which he suffered acutely--in idleness, apparently--and perhaps that was one of the causes of his disorder--he told us at length, but many of the incidents were so evidently worn by the constant handling of his mind that they gave no clear impression.

Finally, he ran away from home, he said. At first he found that a wholly new place and new people took him out of himself ("surprised me," he said, "so that I could not live everything beforehand"). Thus he fled. The slang he used, "chased himself all over the country," seemed peculiarly expressive. He had been in foreign countries; he had herded sheep in Australia (so he said), and certainly from his knowledge of the country he had wandered with the gamboleros of South America; he had gone for gold to Alaska, and worked in the lumber camps of the Pacific Northwest. But he could not escape, he said. In a short time he was no longer "surprised." His account of his travels, while fragmentary, had a peculiar vividness. He *saw* what he described, and he saw it so plainly that his mind ran off into curious details that made his words strike sometimes like flashes of lightning. A strange and wonderful mind--uncontrolled. How that man needed the discipline of common work!

I have rarely listened to a story with such rapt interest. It was not only what he said, nor how he said it, but how he let me see the strange workings of his mind. It was continuously a story of a story. When his voice finally died down I drew a long breath and was astonished to perceive that it was nearly midnight--and Harriet speechless with her emotions. For a moment he sat quiet and then burst out:

"I cannot get away: I cannot escape," and the veritable look of some trapped creature came into his eyes, fear so abject that I reached over and laid my hand on his arm:

"Friend," I said, "stop here. We have a good country. You have travelled far enough. I know from experience what a cornfield will do for a man."

"I have lived all sorts of life," he continued as if he had not heard a word I said, "and I have lived it all twice, and I am afraid."

"Face it," I said, gripping his arm, longing for some power to "blow grit into him."

"Face it!" he exclaimed, "don't you suppose I have tried. If I could do a thing--anything--a few times without thinking-- *once* would be enough--I might be all right. I should be all right."

He brought his fist down on the table, and there was a note of resolution in his voice. I moved my chair nearer to him, feeling as though I were saving an immortal soul from destruction. I told him of our life, how the quiet and the work of it would solve his problems. I sketched with enthusiasm my own experience and I planned swiftly how he could live, absorbed in simple work--and in books.

"Try it," I said eagerly.

"I will," he said, rising from the table, and grasping my hand. "I'll stay here."

I had a peculiar thrill of exultation and triumph. I know how the priest must feel, having won a soul from torment!

He was trembling with excitement and pale with emotion and weariness. One must begin the quiet life with rest. So I got him off to bed, first pouring him a bath-tub of warm water. I laid out clean clothes by his bedside and took away his old ones, talking to him cheerfully all the time about common things. When I finally left him and came downstairs I found Harriet standing with frightened eyes in the middle of the kitchen.

"I'm afraid to have him sleep in this house," she said.

But I reassured her. "You do not understand," I said.

Owing to the excitement of the evening I spent a restless night. Before daylight, while I was dreaming a strange dream of two men running, the one who pursued being the exact counterpart of the one who fled, I heard my name called aloud:

"David, David!"

I sprang out of bed.

"The tramp has gone," called Harriet.

He had not even slept in his bed. He had raised the window, dropped out on the ground and vanished.

X
THE INFIDEL

I find that we have an infidel in this community. I don't know that I should set down the fact here on good white paper; the walls, they say, have eyes, the stones have ears. But consider these words written in bated breath! The worst of it is--I gather from common report--this infidel is a Cheerful Infidel, whereas a true infidel should bear upon his face the living mark of his infamy. We are all tolerant enough of those who do not agree with us, provided only they are sufficiently miserable! I confess when I first heard of him--through Mrs. Horace (with shudders)--I was possessed of a consuming secret desire to see him. I even thought of climbing a tree somewhere along the public road--like Zaccheus, wasn't it?--and watching him go by. If by any chance he should look my way I could easily avoid discovery by crouching among the leaves. It shows how pleasant must be the paths of unrighteousness that we are tempted to climb trees to see those who walk therein. My imagination busied itself with the infidel. I pictured him as a sort of Moloch treading our pleasant countryside, flames and smoke proceeding from his nostrils, his feet striking fire, his voice like the sound of a great wind. At least that was the picture I formed of him from common report.

And yesterday afternoon I met the infidel and I must here set down a true account of the adventure. It is, surely, a little new door opened in the house of my understanding. I might travel a whole year in a city, brushing men's elbows, and not once have such an experience. In country spaces men develop sensitive surfaces, not calloused by too frequent contact, accepting the new impression vividly and keeping it bright to think upon.

I met the infidel as the result of a rather unexpected series of incidents. I don't think I have said before that we have for some time been expecting a great event on this farm. We have raised corn and buckwheat, we have a fertile asparagus bed and onions and pie-plant (enough to supply the entire population of this community) and I can't tell how many other vegetables. We have had plenty of chickens hatched out (I don't like chickens, especially hens, especially a certain gaunt and predatory hen named [so Harriet says] Evangeline, who belongs to a neighbour of ours) and we have had two litters of pigs, but until this bright moment of expectancy we never have had a calf.

Upon the advice of Horace, which I often lean upon as upon a staff, I have been keeping my young heifer shut up in the cow-yard now for a week or two. But yesterday, toward the middle of the afternoon, I found the fence broken down and the cow-yard empty. From what Harriet said, the brown cow must have been gone since early morning. I knew, of course, what that meant, and straightway I took a stout stick and set off over the hill, tracing the brown cow as far as I could by her tracks. She had made way toward a clump of trees near Horace's wood lot, where I confidently expected to find her. But as fate would have it, the pasture gate, which is rarely used, stood open and the tracks led outward into an old road. I followed rapidly, half pleased that I had not found her within the wood. It was a promise of new adventure which I came to with downright enjoyment (confidentially--I should have been cultivating corn!). I peered into every thicket as I passed: once I climbed an old fence and, standing on the top rail, intently surveyed my neighbour's pasture. No brown cow was to be seen. At the crossing of the brook I shouldered my way from the road down a path among the alders, thinking the brown cow might have gone that way to obscurity.

It is curious how, in spite of domestication and training, Nature in her great moments returns to the primitive and instinctive! My brown cow, never having had anything but the kindest treatment, is as gentle an animal as could be imagined, but she had followed the nameless, ages-old law of her breed: she had escaped in her great moment to the most secret place she knew. It did not matter that she would have been safer in my yard--both she and her calf--that she would have been surer of her food; she could only obey the old wild law. So turkeys will hide their nests. So the tame duck, tame for unnumbered generations, hearing from afar the shrill cry of the wild drake, will desert her quiet surroundings, spread her little-used wings and become for a time the wildest of the wild.

So we think--you and I--that we are civilised! But how often, how often, have we felt that old wildness which is our common heritage, scarce shackled, clamouring in our blood!

I stood listening among the alders, in the deep cool shade. Here and there a ray of sunshine came through the thick foliage: I could see it where it silvered the cobweb ladders of those moist spaces. Somewhere in the thicket I heard an unalarmed catbird trilling her exquisite song, a startled frog leaped with a splash into the water; faint odours of some blossoming growth, not distinguishable, filled the still air. It was one of those rare moments when one seems to have caught Nature unaware. I lingered a full minute, listening, looking; but my brown cow had not gone that way. So I turned and went up rapidly to the road, and there I found myself almost face to face with a ruddy little man whose countenance bore a look of round astonishment. We were both surprised. I recovered first.

"Have you seen a brown cow?" I asked.

He was still so astonished that he began to look around him; he thrust his hands nervously into his coat pockets and pulled them out again.

"I think you won't find her in there," I said, seeking to relieve his embarrassment.

But I didn't know, then, how very serious a person I had encountered.

"No--no," he stammered, "I haven't seen your cow."

So I explained to him with sobriety, and at some length, the problem I had to solve. He was greatly interested and inasmuch as he was going my way he offered at once to assist me in my search. So we set off together. He was rather stocky of build, and decidedly short of breath, so that I regulated my customary stride to suit his deliberation. At first, being filled with the spirit of my adventure, I was not altogether pleased with this arrangement. Our conversation ran something like this:

STRANGER: Has she any spots or marks on her?

MYSELF: No, she is plain brown.

STRANGER: How old a cow is she?

MYSELF: This is her first calf.

STRANGER: Valuable animal?

MYSELF: (fencing): I have never put a price on her; she is a promising young heifer.

STRANGER: Pure blood?

MYSELF: No, grade.

After a pause:

STRANGER: Live around here?

MYSELF: Yes, half a mile below here. Do you?

STRANGER: Yes, three miles above here. My name's Purdy.

MYSELF: Mine is Grayson.

He turned to me solemnly and held out his hand. "*I'm* glad to meet you, Mr. Grayson," he said. "And I'm glad," I said, "to meet you, Mr. Purdy."

I will not attempt to put down all we said: I couldn't. But by such devices is the truth in the country made manifest.

So we continued to walk and look. Occasionally I would unconsciously increase my pace until I was warned to desist by the puffing of Mr. Purdy. He gave an essential impression of genial timidity: and how he *did* love to talk!

We came at last to a rough bit of land grown up to scrubby oaks and hazel brush.

"This," said Mr. Purdy, "looks hopeful."

We followed the old road, examining every bare spot of earth for some evidence of the cow's tracks, but without finding so much as a sign. I was for pushing onward but Mr. Purdy insisted that this clump of woods was exactly such a place as a cow would like. He developed such a capacity for argumentation and seemed so sure of what he was talking about that I yielded, and we entered the wood.

"We'll part here," he said: "you keep over there about fifty yards and I'll go straight ahead. In that way we'll cover the ground. Keep a-shoutin'."

So we started and I kept a-shoutin'. He would answer from time to time: "Hulloo hulloo!"

It was a wild and beautiful bit of forest. The ground under the trees was thickly covered with enormous ferns or bracken, with here and there patches of light where the sun came through the foliage. The low spots were filled with the coarse green verdure of skunk cabbage. I was so sceptical about finding the cow in a wood where concealment was so easy that I confess I rather idled and enjoyed the surroundings. Suddenly, however, I heard Mr. Purdy's voice, with a new note in it:

"Hulloo, hulloo----"

"What luck?"

"Hulloo, hulloo----"

"I'm coming--" and I turned and ran as rapidly as I could through the trees, jumping over logs and dodging low branches, wondering what new thing my friend had discovered. So I came to his side.

"Have you got trace of her?" I questioned eagerly.

"Sh!" he said, "over there. Don't you see her?"

"Where, where?"

He pointed, but for a moment I could see nothing but the trees and the bracken. Then all at once, like the puzzle in a picture, I saw her plainly. She was standing perfectly motionless, her head lowered, and in such a peculiar clump of bushes and ferns that she was all but indistinguishable. It was wonderful, the perfection with which her instinct had led her to conceal herself.

All excitement, I started toward her at once. But Mr. Purdy put his hand on my arm.

"Wait," he said, "don't frighten her. She has her calf there."

"No!" I exclaimed, for I could see nothing of it.

We went, cautiously, a few steps nearer. She threw up her head and looked at us so wildly for a moment that I should hardly have known her for my cow. She was, indeed, for the time being, a wild creature of the wood. She made a low sound and advanced a step threateningly.

"Steady," said Mr. Purdy, "this is her first calf. Stop a minute and keep quiet. She'll soon get used to us."

Moving to one side cautiously, we sat down on an old log. The brown heifer paused, every muscle tense, her eyes literally blazing, We sat perfectly still. After a minute or two she lowered her head, and with curious guttural sounds she began to lick her calf, which lay quite hidden in the bracken.

"She has chosen a perfect spot," I thought to myself, for it was the wildest bit of forest I had seen anywhere in this neighbourhood. At one side, not far off, rose a huge gray rock, partly covered on one side with moss, and round about were oaks and a few ash trees of a poor scrubby sort (else they would long ago have been cut out). The earth underneath was soft and springy with leaf mould.--

Mr. Purdy was one to whom silence was painful; he fidgeted about, evidently bursting with talk, and yet feeling compelled to follow his own injunction of silence. Presently he reached into his capacious pocket and handed me a little paper-covered booklet. I took it, curious, and read the title:

"Is There a Hell?"

It struck me humorously. In the country we are always--at least some of us are--more or less in a religious ferment, The city may distract itself to the point where faith is unnecessary; but in the country we must, perforce, have something to believe in. And we talk about it, too! I read the title aloud, but in a low voice:

"Is There a Hell?" Then I asked: "Do you really want to know?"

"The argument is all there," he replied.

"Well," I said, "I can tell you off-hand, out of my own experience, that there certainly is a hell----"

He turned toward me with evident astonishment, but I proceeded with tranquillity:

"Yes, sir, there's no doubt about it. I've been near enough myself several times to smell the smoke. It isn't around here," I said.

As he looked at me his china-blue eyes grew larger, if that were possible, and his serious, gentle face took on a look of pained surprise.

"Before you say such things," he said, "I beg you to read my book."

He took the tract from my hands and opened it on his knee.

"The Bible tells us," he said, "that in the beginning God created the heavens and the earth, He made the firmament and divided the waters. But does the Bible say that He created a hell or a devil? Does it?"

I shook my head.

"Well, then!" he said triumphantly, "and that isn't all, either. The historian Moses gives in detail a full account of what was made in six days. He tells how day and night were created, how the sun and the moon and the stars were made; he tells how God created the flowers of the field, and the insects, and the birds, and the great whales, and said, 'Be fruitful and multiply,' He accounts for every minute of the time in the entire six days--and of course God rested on the seventh--and there is not one word about hell. Is there?"

I shook my head.

"Well then--" exultantly, "where is it? I'd like to have any man, no matter how wise he is, answer that. Where is it?"

"That," I said, "has troubled me, too. We don't always know just where our hells are. If we did we might avoid them. We are not so sensitive to them as we should be--do you think?"

He looked at me intently: I went on before he could answer:

"Why, I've seen men in my time living from day to day in the very atmosphere of perpetual torment, and actually arguing that there was no hell. It is a strange sight, I assure you, and one that will trouble you afterwards. From what I know of hell, it is a place of very loose boundaries. Sometimes I've thought we couldn't be quite sure when we were in it and when we were not."

I did not tell my friend, but I was thinking of the remark of old Swedenborg: "The trouble with hell is we shall not know it when we arrive."

At this point Mr. Purdy burst out again, having opened his little book at another page.

"When Adam and Eve had sinned," he said, "and the God of Heaven walked in the garden in the cool of the evening and called for them and they had hidden themselves on account of their disobedience, did God say to them: Unless you repent of your sins and get forgiveness I will shut you up in yon dark and dismal hell and torment you (or have the devil do it) for ever and ever? Was there such a word?"

I shook my head.

"No, sir," he said vehemently, "there was not."

"But does it say," I asked, "that Adam and Eve had not themselves been using their best wits in creating a hell? That point has occurred to me. In my experience I've known both Adams and Eves who were most adroit in their capacity for making places of torment--and afterwards of getting into them. Just watch yourself some day after you've sown a crop of desires and you'll see promising little hells starting up within you like pigweeds and pusley after a warm rain in your garden. And our heavens, too, for that matter--they grow to our own planting: and how sensitive they are too! How soon the hot wind of a passion withers them away! How surely the fires of selfishness blacken their perfection!"

I'd almost forgotten Mr. Purdy--and when I looked around, his face wore a peculiar puzzled expression not unmixed with alarm. He held up his little book eagerly almost in my face.

"If God had intended to create a hell," he said, "I assert without fear of success-ful contradiction that when God was there in the Garden of Eden it was the time for Him to have put Adam and Eve and all their posterity on notice that there was a place of everlasting torment. It would have been only a square deal for Him to do so. But did He?"

I shook my head.

"He did not. If He had mentioned hell on that occasion I should not now dis-pute its existence. But He did not. This is what He said to Adam--the very words: 'In the sweat of thy face shalt thou eat bread, till thou return unto the ground: for out of it thou wast taken: for dust thou art, and unto dust shalt thou return.' You see He did not say 'Unto hell shalt thou return.' He said, 'Unto dust.' That isn't hell, is it?"

"Well," I said, "there are in my experience a great many different kinds of hells. There are almost as many kinds of hells as there are men and women upon this earth. Now, your hell wouldn't terrify me in the least. My own makes me no end of trouble. Talk about burning pitch and brimstone: how futile were the imagina-tions of the old fellows who conjured up such puerile torments. Why, I can tell you of no end of hells that are worse--and not half try. Once I remember, when I was younger----"

I happened to glance around at my companion. He sat there looking at me with horror--fascinated horror.

"Well, I won't disturb your peace of mind by telling *that* story," I said.

"Do you believe that we shall go to hell?" he asked in a low voice.

"That depends," I said. "Let's leave out the question of 'we'; let's be more com-fortably general in our discussion. I think we can safely say that some go and some do not. It's a curious and noteworthy thing," I said, "but I've known of cases--There are some people who aren't really worth good honest tormenting--let alone the rewards of heavenly bliss. They just haven't anything to torment! What is going to become of such folks? I confess I don't know. You remember when Dante began his journey into the infernal regions----"

"I don't believe a word of that Dante," he interrupted excitedly; "it's all a made up story. There isn't a word of truth in it; it is a blasphemous book. Let me read you what I say about it in here."

"I will agree with you without argument," I said, "that it is not *all* true. I merely wanted to speak of one of Dante's experiences as an illustration of the point I'm making. You remember that almost the first spirits he met on his journey were those who had never done anything in this life to merit either heaven or hell. That always struck me as being about the worst plight imaginable for a human being. Think of a creature not even worth good honest brimstone!"

Since I came home, I've looked up the passage; and it is a wonderful one. Dante heard wailings and groans and terrible things said in many tongues. Yet these were not the souls of the wicked. They were only those "who had lived without praise or blame, thinking of nothing but themselves." "Heaven would not dull its brightness with those, nor would lower hell receive them."

"And what is it," asked Dante, "that makes them so grievously suffer?"

"Hopelessness of death," said Virgil, "Their blind existence here, and immemorable former life, make them so wretched that they envy every other lot. Mercy and Justice alike disdain them. Let us speak of them no more. Look, and pass!"

But Mr. Purdy, in spite of his timidity, was a man of much persistence.

"They tell me," he said, "when they try to prove the reasonableness of hell, that unless you show sinners how they're goin' to be tormented, they'd never repent. Now, I say that if a man has to be scared into religion, his religion ain't much good."

"There," I said, "I agree with you completely."

His face lighted up, and he continued eagerly:

"And I tell 'em: You just go ahead and try for heaven; don't pay any attention to all this talk about everlasting punishment."

"Good advice!" I said.

It had begun to grow dark. The brown cow was quiet at last. We could hear small faint sounds from the calf. I started slowly through the bracken. Mr. Purdy hung at my elbow, stumbling sideways as he walked, but continuing to talk eagerly. So we came to the place where the calf lay. I spoke in a low voice:

"So boss, so boss."

I would have laid my hand on her neck but she started back with a wild toss of her horns. It was a beautiful calf! I looked at it with a peculiar feeling of exultation, pride, ownership. It was red-brown, with a round curly pate and one white leg. As it lay curled there among the ferns, it was really beautiful to look at. When we approached, it did not so much as stir. I lifted it to its legs, upon which the cow uttered a strange half-wild cry and ran a few steps off, her head thrown in the air. The calf fell back as though it had no legs.

"She is telling it not to stand up," said Mr. Purdy.

I had been afraid at first that something was the matter!

"Some are like that," he said. "Some call their calves to run. Others won't let you come near 'em at all; and I've even known of a case where a cow gored its calf to death rather than let anyone touch it."

I looked at Mr. Purdy not without a feeling of admiration. This was a thing he knew: a language not taught in the universities. How well it became him to know it; how simply he expressed it! I thought to myself: There are not many men in this world, after all, that it will not pay us to go to school to--for something or other.

I should never have been able, indeed, to get the cow and calf home, last night at least, if it had not been for my chance friend. He knew exactly what to do and how to do it. He wore a stout coat of denim, rather long in the skirts. This he slipped off, while I looked on in some astonishment, and spread it out on the ground. He placed my staff under one side of it and found another stick nearly the same size for the other side. These he wound into the coat until he had made a sort of stretcher. Upon this we placed the unresisting calf. What a fine one it was! Then, he in front and I behind, we carried the stretcher and its burden out of the wood. The cow followed, sometimes threatening, sometimes bellowing, sometimes starting off wildly, head and tail in the air, only to rush back and, venturing up with trembling muscles, touch her tongue to the calf, uttering low maternal sounds.

"Keep steady," said Mr. Purdy, "and everything'll be all right."

When we came to the brook we stopped to rest. I think my companion would have liked to start his argument again, but he was too short of breath.

It was a prime spring evening! The frogs were tuning up. I heard a drowsy cowbell somewhere over the hills in the pasture. The brown cow, with eager, outstretched neck, was licking her calf as it lay there on the improvised stretcher. I looked up at the sky, a blue avenue of heaven between the tree tops; I felt the peculiar sense of mystery which nature so commonly conveys.

"I have been too sure!" I said. "What do we know after all! Why may there not be future heavens and hells--'other heavens for other earths'? We do not know--we do not ***know***--"

So, carrying the calf, in the cool of the evening, we came at last to my yard. We had no sooner put the calf down than it jumped nimbly to its feet and ran, wobbling absurdly, to meet its mother.

"The rascal," I said, "after all our work."

"It's the nature of the animal," said Mr. Purdy, as he put on his coat.

I could not thank him enough. I invited him to stay with us to supper, but he said he must hurry home.

"Then come down soon to see me," I said, "and we will settle this question as to the existence of a hell."

He stepped up close to me and said, with an appealing note in his voice:

"You do not really believe in a hell, do you?"

How human nature loves collusiveness: nothing short of the categorical will satisfy us! What I said to Mr. Purdy evidently appeased him, for he seized my hand and shook and shook.

"We haven't understood each other," he said eagerly. "You don't believe in eternal damnation any more than I do." Then he added, as though some new uncertainty puzzled him, "Do you?"

At supper I was telling Harriet with gusto of my experiences. Suddenly she broke out:

"What was his name?"

"Purdy."

"Why, he's the infidel that Mrs. Horace tells about!"

"Is that possible?" I said, and I dropped my knife and fork. The strangest sensation came over me.

"Why," I said, "then I'm an infidel too!"

So I laughed and I've been laughing gloriously ever since--at myself, at the infidel, at the entire neighbourhood. I recalled that delightful character in "The Vicar of Wakefield" (my friend the Scotch Preacher loves to tell about him), who seasons error by crying out "Fudge!"

"Fudge!" I said.

We're all poor sinners!

XI
THE COUNTRY DOCTOR

Sunday afternoon, June 9.

We had a funeral to-day in this community and the longest funeral procession, Charles Baxter says, he has seen in all the years of his memory among these hills. A good man has gone away--and yet remains. In the comparatively short time I have been here I never came to know him well personally, though I saw him often in the country roads, a ruddy old gentleman with thick, coarse, iron-gray hair, somewhat stern of countenance, somewhat shabby of attire, sitting as erect as a trooper in his open buggy, one muscular hand resting on his knee, the other holding the reins of his familiar old white horse. I said I did not come to know him well personally, and yet no one who knows this community can help knowing Doctor John North. I never so desired the gift of moving expression as I do at this moment, on my return from his funeral, that I may give some faint idea of what a good man means to a community like ours--as the more complete knowledge of it has come to me to-day.

In the district school that I attended when a boy we used to love to leave our mark, as we called it, wherever our rovings led us. It was a bit of boyish mysticism, unaccountable now that we have grown older and wiser (perhaps); but it had its meaning. It was an instinctive outreaching of the young soul to perpetuate the knowledge of its existence upon this forgetful earth. My mark, I remember, was a notch and a cross. With what secret fond diligence I carved it in the gray bark of beech trees, on fence posts, or on barn doors, and once, I remember, on the roof-ridge of our home, and once, with high imaginings of how long it would remain, I spent hours chiseling it deep in a hard-headed old boulder in the pasture, where, if man has been as kind as Nature, it remains to this day. If you should chance to see it you would not know of the boy who carved it there.

So Doctor North left his secret mark upon the neighbourhood--as all of us do, for good or for ill, upon **our** neighbourhoods, in accordance with the strength of that character which abides within us. For a long time I did not know that it was he, though it was not difficult to see that some strong good man had often passed this way. I saw the mystic sign of him deep-lettered in the hearthstone of a home; I heard it speaking bravely from the weak lips of a friend; it is carved in the plastic heart of many a boy. No, I do not doubt the immortalities of the soul; in this community, which I have come to love so much, dwells more than one of John North's immortalities--and will continue to dwell. I, too, live more deeply because John North was here.

He was in no outward way an extraordinary man, nor was his life eventful. He was born in this neighbourhood: I saw him lying quite still this morning in the same sunny room of the same house where he first saw the light of day. Here among these common hills he grew up, and save for the few years he spent at school or in the army, he lived here all his life long. In old neighbourhoods and especially farm neighbourhoods people come to know one another--not clothes knowledge, or money knowledge--but that sort of knowledge which reaches down into the hidden springs of human character. A country community may be deceived by a stranger, too easily deceived, but not by one of its own people. For it is not a studied knowledge; it resembles that slow geologic uncovering before which not even the deep buried bones of the prehistoric saurian remain finally hidden.

I never fully realised until this morning what a supreme triumph it is, having grown old, to merit the respect of those who know us best. Mere greatness offers no reward to compare with it, for greatness compels that homage which we freely bestow upon goodness. So long as I live I shall never forget this morning. I stood in the door-yard outside of the open window of the old doctor's home. It was soft, and warm, and very still--a June Sunday morning. An apple tree not far off was still in blossom, and across the road on a grassy hillside sheep fed unconcernedly. Occasionally, from the roadway where the horses of the countryside were waiting, I heard the clink of a bit-ring or the low voice of some new-comer seeking a place to hitch. Not half those who came could find room in the house: they stood uncovered among the trees. From within, wafted through the window, came the faint odour of flowers, and the occasional minor intonation of someone speaking--and finally our own Scotch Preacher! I could not see him, but there lay in the cadences of his voice a peculiar note of peacefulness, of finality. The day before he died Dr. North had said:

"I want McAlway to conduct my funeral, not as a minister but as a man. He has been my friend for forty years; he will know what I mean."

The Scotch Preacher did not say much. Why should he? Everyone there *knew*: and speech would only have cheapened what we knew. And I do not now recall even the little he said, for there was so much all about me that spoke not of the death of a good man, but of his life. A boy who stood near me--a boy no longer, for he was as tall as a man--gave a more eloquent tribute than any preacher could have done. I saw him stand his ground for a time with that grim courage of youth which dreads emotion more than a battle: and then I saw him crying behind a tree! He was not a relative of the old doctor's; he was only one of many into whose deep life the doctor had entered.

They sang "Lead, Kindly Light," and came out through the narrow doorway into the sunshine with the coffin, the hats of the pallbearers in a row on top, and there was hardly a dry eye among us.

And as they came out through the narrow doorway, I thought how the Doctor must have looked out daily through so many, many years upon this beauty of hills and fields and of sky above, grown dearer from long familiarity--which he would know no more. And Kate North, the Doctor's sister, his only relative, followed behind, her fine old face gray and set, but without a tear in her eye. How like the Doctor she looked: the same stern control!

In the hours which followed, on the pleasant winding way to the cemetery, in the groups under the trees, on the way homeward again, the community spoke its true heart, and I have come back with the feeling that human nature, at bottom, is sound and sweet. I knew a great deal before about Doctor North, but I knew it as knowledge, not as emotion, and therefore it was not really a part of my life.

I heard again the stories of how he drove the country roads, winter and summer, how he had seen most of the population into the world and had held the hands of many who went out! It was the plain, hard life of a country doctor, and yet it seemed to rise in our community like some great tree, its roots deep buried in the soil of our common life, its branches close to the sky. To those accustomed to the outward excitements of city life it would have seemed barren and uneventful. It was significant that the talk was not so much of what the Doctor did as of *how* he did it, not so much of his actions as of the natural expression of his character. And when we come to think of it, goodness *is* uneventful. It does not flash, it glows. It is deep, quiet and very simple. It passes not with oratory, it is commonly foreign to riches, nor does it often sit in the places of the mighty: but may be felt in the touch of a friendly hand or the look of a kindly eye.

Outwardly, John North often gave the impression of brusqueness. Many a woman, going to him for the first time, and until she learned that he was in reality as gentle as a girl, was frightened by his manner. The country is full of stories of such encounters. We laugh yet over the adventure of a woman who formerly came to spend her summers here. She dressed very beautifully and was "nervous." One day she went to call on the Doctor. He made a careful examination and asked many questions. Finally he said, with portentous solemnity:

"Madam, you're suffering from a very common complaint."

The Doctor paused, then continued, impressively:

"You haven't enough work to do. This is what I would advise. Go home, discharge your servants, do your own cooking, wash your own clothes and make your own beds. You'll get well."

She is reported to have been much offended, and yet to-day there was a wreath of white roses in Doctor North's room sent from the city by that woman.

If he really hated anything in this world the Doctor hated whimperers. He had a deep sense of the purpose and need of punishment, and he despised those who fled from wholesome discipline.

A young fellow once went to the Doctor--so they tell the story--and asked for something to stop his pain.

"Stop it!" exclaimed the Doctor: "why, it's good for you. You've done wrong, haven't you? Well, you're being punished; take it like a man. There's nothing more wholesome than good honest pain."

And yet how much pain he alleviated in this community--in forty years!

The deep sense that a man should stand up to his fate was one of the key-notes of his character; and the way he taught it, not only by word but by every action of his life, put heart into many a weak man and woman, Mrs. Patterson, a friend of ours, tells of a reply she once had from the Doctor to whom she had gone with a new trouble. After telling him about it she said:

"I've left it all with the Lord."

"You'd have done better," said the Doctor, "to keep it yourself. Trouble is for your discipline: the Lord doesn't need it."

It was thus out of his wisdom that he was always telling people what they knew, deep down in their hearts, to be true. It sometimes hurt at first, but sooner or later, if the man had a spark of real manhood in him, he came back, and gave the Doctor an abiding affection.

There were those who, though they loved him, called him intolerant. I never could look at it that way. He *did* have the only kind of intolerance which is at all tolerable, and that is the intolerance of intolerance. He always set himself with vigour against that unreason and lack of sympathy which are the essence of intolerance; and yet there was a rock of conviction on many subjects behind which he could not be driven. It was not intolerance: it was with him a reasoned certainty of belief. He had a phrase to express that not uncommon state of mind in this age particularly, which is politely willing to yield its foothold within this universe to almost any reasoner who suggests some other universe, however shadowy, to stand upon. He called it a "mush of concession." He might have been wrong in his convictions, but he, at least, never floundered in a "mush of concession." I heard him say once:

"There are some things a man can't concede, and one is, that a man who has broken a law, like a man who has broken a leg, has got to suffer for it."

It was only with the greatest difficulty that he could be prevailed upon to present a bill. It was not because the community was poor, though some of our people are poor, and it was certainly not because the Doctor was rich and could afford such philanthropy, for, saving a rather unproductive farm which during the last ten years of his life lay wholly uncultivated, he was as poor as any man in the community. He simply seemed to forget that people owed him.

It came to be a common and humorous experience for people to go to the Doctor and say:

"Now, Doctor North, how much do I owe you? You remember you attended my wife two years ago when the baby came--and John when he had the diphtheria----"

"Yes, yes," said the Doctor, "I remember."

"I thought I ought to pay you."

"Well, I'll look it up when I get time."

But he wouldn't. The only way was to go to him and say:

"Doctor, I want to pay ten dollars on account."

"All right," he'd answer, and take the money.

To the credit of the community I may say with truthfulness that the Doctor never suffered. He was even able to supply himself with the best instruments that money could buy. To him nothing was too good for our neighbourhood. This morning I saw in a case at his home a complete set of oculist's instruments, said to be the best in the county--a very unusual equipment for a country doctor. Indeed, he assumed that the responsibility for the health of the community rested upon him. He was a sort of self-constituted health officer. He was always sniffing about for old wells and damp cellars--and somehow, with his crisp humour and sound sense, getting them cleaned. In his old age he even grew querulously particular about these things--asking a little more of human nature than it could quite accomplish. There were innumerable other ways--how they came out to-day all glorified now that he is gone!--in which he served the community.

Horace tells how he once met the Doctor driving his old white horse in the town road.

"Horace," called the Doctor, "why don't you paint your barn?"

"Well," said Horace, "it *is* beginning to look a bit shabby."

"Horace," said the Doctor, "you're a prominent citizen. We look to you to keep up the credit of the neighbourhood."

Horace painted his barn.

I think Doctor North was fonder of Charles Baxter than of anyone else, save his sister. He hated sham and cant: if a man had a single *reality* in him the old Doctor found it; and Charles Baxter in many ways exceeds any man I ever knew in the downright quality of genuineness. The Doctor was never tired of telling--and with humour--how he once went to Baxter to have a table made for his office. When he came to get it he found the table upside clown and Baxter on his knees finishing off the under part of the drawer slides. Baxter looked up and smiled in the engaging way he has, and continued his work. After watching him for some time the Doctor said:

"Baxter, why do you spend so much time on that table? Who's going to know whether or not the last touch has been put on the under side of it?"

Baxter straightened up and looked at the Doctor in surprise.

"Why, I will," he said.

How the Doctor loved to tell that story! I warrant there is no boy who ever grew up in this country who hasn't heard it.

It was a part of his pride in finding reality that made the Doctor such a lover of true sentiment and such a hater of sentimentality. I prize one memory of him which illustrates this point. The district school gave a "speaking" and we all went. One boy with a fresh young voice spoke a "soldier piece"--the soliloquy of a one-armed veteran who sits at a window and sees the troops go by with dancing banners and glittering bayonets, and the people cheering and shouting. And the refrain went something like this:

"Never again call 'Comrade' To the men who were comrades for years; Never again call 'Brother' To the men we think of with tears."

I happened to look around while the boy was speaking, and there sat the old Doctor with the tears rolling unheeded down his ruddy face; he was thinking, no doubt, of *his* war time and the comrades *he* knew.

On the other hand, how he despised fustian and bombast. His "Bah!" delivered explosively, was often like a breath of fresh air in a stuffy room. Several years ago, before I came here--and it is one of the historic stories of the county--there was a semi-political Fourth of July celebration with a number of ambitious orators. One of them, a young fellow of small worth who wanted to be elected to the legislature, made an impassioned address on "Patriotism." The Doctor was present, for he liked gatherings: he liked people. But he did not like the young orator, and did not want him to be elected. In the midst of the speech, while the audience was being carried through the clouds of oratory, the Doctor was seen to be growing more and more uneasy. Finally he burst out:

"Bah!"

The orator caught himself, and then swept on again.

"Bah!" said the Doctor.

By this time the audience was really interested. The orator stopped. He knew the Doctor, and he should have known better than to say what he did. But he was very young and he knew the Doctor was opposing him.

"Perhaps," he remarked sarcastically, "the Doctor can make a better speech than I can."

The Doctor rose instantly, to his full height--and he was an impressive-looking man.

"Perhaps," he said, "I can, and what is more, I will." He stood up on a chair and gave them a talk on Patriotism--real patriotism--the patriotism of duty done in the small concerns of life. That speech, which ended the political career of the orator, is not forgotten to-day.

One thing I heard to-day about the old Doctor impressed me deeply. I have been thinking about it ever since: it illuminates his character more than anything I have heard. It is singular, too, that I should not have known the story before. I don't believe it was because it all happened so long ago; it rather remained untold out of deference to a sort of neighbourhood delicacy.

I had, indeed, wondered why a man of such capacities, so many qualities of real greatness and power, should have escaped a city career. I said something to this effect to a group of men with whom I was talking this morning. I thought they exchanged glances; one said:

"When he first came out of the army he'd made such a fine record as a surgeon that everyone-urged him to go to the city and practice----"

A pause followed which no one seemed inclined to fill.

"But he didn't go," I said.

"No, he didn't go. He was a brilliant young fellow. He *knew* a lot, and he was popular, too. He'd have had a great success----"

Another pause.

"But he didn't go?" I asked promptingly.

"No; he staid here. He was better educated than any man in this county. Why, I've seen him more'n once pick up a book of Latin and read it *for pleasure*."

I could see that all this was purposely irrelevant, and I liked them for it. But walking home from the cemetery Horace gave me the story; the community knew it to the last detail. I suppose it is a story not uncommon among men, but this morning, told of the old Doctor we had just laid away, it struck me with a tragic poignancy difficult to describe.

"Yes," said Horace, "he was to have been married, forty years ago, and the match was broken off because he was a drunkard."

"A drunkard!" I exclaimed, with a shock I cannot convey.

"Yes, sir," said Horace, "one o' the worst you ever see. He got it in the army. Handsome, wild, brilliant--that was the Doctor. I was a little boy but I remember it mighty well."

He told me the whole distressing story. It was all a long time ago and the details do not matter now. It was to be expected that a man like the old Doctor should love, love once, and love as few men do. And that is what he did--and the girl left him because he was a drunkard!

"They all thought," said Horace, "that he'd up an' kill himself. He said he would, but he didn't. Instid o' that he put an open bottle on his table and he looked at it and said: 'Which is stronger, now, you or John North? We'll make that the test,' he said, 'we'll live or die by that.' Them was his exact words. He couldn't sleep nights and he got haggard like a sick man, but he left the bottle there and never touched it."

How my heart throbbed with the thought of that old silent struggle! How much it explained; how near it brought all these people around him! It made him so human. It is the tragic necessity (but the salvation) of many a man that he should come finally to an irretrievable experience, to the assurance that everything is lost. For with that moment, if he be strong, he is saved. I wonder if anyone ever attains real human sympathy who has not passed through the fire of some such experience. Or to humour either! For in the best laughter do we not hear constantly that deep minor note which speaks of the ache in the human heart? It seems to me I can understand Doctor North!

He died Friday morning. He had been lying very quiet all night; suddenly he opened his eyes and said to his sister: "Good-bye, Kate," and shut them again. That was all. The last call had come and he was ready for it. I looked at his face after death. I saw the iron lines of that old struggle in his mouth and chin; and the humour that it brought him in the lines around his deep-set eyes.

----And as I think of him this afternoon, I can see him--curiously, for I can hardly explain it--carrying a banner as in battle right here among our quiet hills. And those he leads seem to be the people we know, the men, and the women, and the boys! He is the hero of a new age. In olden days he might have been a pioneer, carrying the light of civilisation to a new land; here he has been a sort of moral pioneer--a pioneering far more difficult than any we have ever known. There are no heroics connected with it, the name of the pioneer will not go ringing down the ages; for it is a silent leadership and its success is measured by victories in other lives. We see it now, only too dimly, when he is gone. We reflect sadly that we did not stop to thank him. How busy we were with our own affairs when he was among us! I wonder is there anyone here to take up the banner he has laid down!

----I forgot to say that the Scotch Preacher chose the most impressive text in the Bible for his talk at the funeral:

"He that is greatest among you, let him be ... as he that doth serve."

And we came away with a nameless, aching sense of loss, thinking how, perhaps, in a small way, we might do something for somebody else--as the old Doctor did.

XII
AN EVENING AT HOME

"How calm and quiet a delight Is it, alone, To read and meditate and write,
By none offended, and offending none. To walk, ride, sit or sleep at one's
own ease, And, pleasing a man's self, none other to displease."

-- *Charles Cotton, a friend of Izaak Walton*, 1650

During the last few months so many of the real adventures of life have
been out of doors and so much of the beauty, too, that I have scarcely
written a word about my books. In the summer the days are so long and
the work so engrossing that a farmer is quite willing to sit quietly on his
porch after supper and watch the long evenings fall--and rest his tired back, and go
to bed early. But the winter is the true time for indoor enjoyment!

Days like these! A cold night after a cold day! Well wrapped, you have made
arctic explorations to the stable, the chicken-yard and the pig-pen; you have dug
your way energetically to the front gate, stopping every few minutes to beat your
arms around your shoulders and watch the white plume of your breath in the still
air--and you have rushed in gladly to the warmth of the dining-room and the lamp-
lit supper. After such a day how sharp your appetite, how good the taste of food!
Harriet's brown bread (moist, with thick, sweet, dark crusts) was never quite so
delicious, and when the meal is finished you push back your chair feeling like a sort
of lord.

"That was a good supper, Harriet," you say expansively.

"Was it?" she asks modestly, but with evident pleasure.

"Cookery," you remark, "is the greatest art in the world----"

"Oh, you were hungry!"

"Next to poetry," you conclude, "and much better appreciated. Think how easy it is to find a poet who will turn you a presentable sonnet, and how very difficult it is to find a cook who will turn you an edible beefsteak----"

I said a good deal more on this subject which I shall not attempt to repeat. Harriet did not listen through it all. She knows what I am capable of when I really get started; and she has her well-defined limits. A practical person, Harriet! When I have gone about so far, she begins clearing the table or takes up her mending--but I don't mind it at all. Having begun talking, it is wonderful how pleasant one's own voice becomes. And think of having a clear field--and no interruptions!

My own particular room, where I am permitted to revel in the desert of my own disorder, opens comfortably off the sitting-room. A lamp with a green shade stands invitingly on the table shedding a circle of light on the books and papers underneath, but leaving all the remainder of the room in dim pleasantness. At one side stands a comfortable big chair with everything in arm's reach, including my note books and ink bottle. Where I sit I can look out through the open doorway and see Harriet near the fireplace rocking and sewing. Sometimes she hums a little tune which I never confess to hearing, lest I miss some of the unconscious cadences. Let the wind blow outside and the snow drift in piles around the doorway and the blinds rattle--I have before me a whole long pleasant evening.

*   *   *   *   *

What a convenient and delightful world is this world of books!--if you bring to it not the obligations of the student, or look upon it as an opiate for idleness, but enter it rather with the enthusiasm of the adventurer! It has vast advantages over the ordinary world of daylight, of barter and trade, of work and worry. In this world every man is his own King--the sort of King one loves to imagine, not concerned in such petty matters as wars and parliaments and taxes, but a mellow and moderate despot who is a true patron of genius--a mild old chap who has in his court the greatest men and women in the world--and all of them vying to please the most vagrant of his moods! Invite any one of them to talk, and if your highness is not pleased with him you have only to put him back in his corner--and bring some jester to sharpen the laughter of your highness, or some poet to set your faintest emotion to music!

I have marked a certain servility in books. They entreat you for a hearing: they cry out from their cases--like men, in an eternal struggle for survival, for immortality.

"Take me," pleads this one, "I am responsive to every mood. You will find in me love and hate, virtue and vice. I don't preach: I give you life as it is. You will find here adventures cunningly linked with romance and seasoned to suit the most fastidious taste. Try *me*."

"Hear such talk!" cries his neighbour. "He's fiction. What he says never happened at all. He tries hard to make you believe it, but it isn't true, not a word of it. Now, I'm fact. Everything you find in me can be depended upon."

"Yes," responds the other, "but who cares! Nobody wants to read you, you're dull."

"You're false!"

As their voices grow shriller with argument your highness listens with the indulgent smile of royalty when its courtiers contend for its favour, knowing that their very life depends upon a wrinkle in your august brow.

*   *   *   *   *

As for me I confess to being a rather crusty despot. When Horace was over here the other evening talking learnedly about silos and ensilage I admit that I became the very pattern of humility, but when I take my place in the throne of my arm-chair with the light from the green-shaded lamp falling on the open pages of my book, I assure you I am decidedly an autocratic person. My retainers must distinctly keep their places! I have my court favourites upon whom I lavish the richest gifts of my attention. I reserve for them a special place in the worn case nearest my person, where at the mere outreaching of an idle hand I can summon them to beguile my moods. The necessary slavies of literature I have arranged in indistinct rows at the farther end of the room where they can be had if I require their special accomplishments.

*   *   *   *   *

How little, after all, learning counts in this world either in books or in men. I have often been awed by the wealth of information I have discovered in a man or a book: I have been awed and depressed. How wonderful, I have thought, that one brain should hold so much, should be so infallible in a world of fallibility. But I have observed how soon and completely such a fount of information dissipates itself. Having only things to give, it comes finally to the end of its things: it is empty. What it has hived up so painfully through many a studious year comes now to be common property. We pass that way, take our share, and do not even say "Thank you." Learning is like money; it is of prodigious satisfaction to the possessor thereof, but once given forth it diffuses itself swiftly.

"What have you?" we are ever asking of those we meet. "Information, learning, money?"

We take it cruelly and pass onward, for such is the law of material possessions.

"What have you?" we ask. "Charm, personality, character, the great gift of unexpectedness?"

How we draw you to us! We take you in. Poor or ignorant though you may be, we link arms and loiter; we love you not for what you have or what you give us, but for what you are.

I have several good friends (excellent people) who act always as I expect them to act. There is no flight! More than once I have listened to the edifying conversation of a certain sturdy old gentleman whom I know, and I am ashamed to say that I have thought:

"Lord! if he would jump up now and turn an intellectual handspring, or slap me on the back (figuratively, of course: the other would be unthinkable), or--yes, swear! I--think I could love him."

But he never does--and I'm afraid he never will!

When I speak then of my books you will know what I mean. The chief charm of literature, old or new, lies in its high quality of surprise, unexpectedness, sponta-neity: high spirits applied to life. We can fairly hear some of the old chaps you and I know laughing down through the centuries. How we love 'em! They laughed for themselves, not for us!

Yes, there must be surprise in the books that I keep in the worn case at my elbow, the surprise of a new personality perceiving for the first time the beauty, the wonder, the humour, the tragedy, the greatness of truth. It doesn't matter at all whether the writer is a poet, a scientist, a traveller, an essayist or a mere daily space-maker, if he have the God-given grace of wonder.

"What on *earth* are you laughing about?" cries Harriet from the sitting-room.

When I have caught my breath, I say, holding up my book:

"This absurd man here is telling of the adventures of a certain chivalrous Knight."

"But I can't see how you can laugh out like that, sitting all alone there. Why, it's uncanny."

"You don't know the Knight, Harriet, nor his squire Sancho."

"You talk of them just as though they were real persons."

"Real!" I exclaim, "real! Why they are much more real than most of the people we know. Horace is a mere wraith compared with Sancho."

And then I rush out.

"Let me read you this," I say, and I read that matchless chapter wherein the Knight, having clapped on his head the helmet which Sancho has inadvertently used as a receptacle for a dinner of curds and, sweating whey profusely, goes forth to fight two fierce lions. As I proceed with that prodigious story, I can see Harriet gradually forgetting her sewing, and I read on the more furiously until, coming to the point of the conflict wherein the generous and gentle lion, having yawned, "threw out some half yard of tongue wherewith he licked and washed his face," Harriet begins to laugh.

"There!" I say triumphantly.

Harriet looks at me accusingly.

"Such foolishness!" she says. "Why should any man in his senses try to fight caged lions!"

"Harriet," I say, "you are incorrigible."

She does not deign to reply, so I return with meekness to my room.

*   *   *   *   *

The most distressing thing about the ordinary fact writer is his cock-sureness. Why, here is a man (I have not yet dropped him out of the window) who has written a large and sober book explaining life. And do you know when he gets through he is apparently much discouraged about this universe. This is the veritable moment when I am in love with my occupation as a despot! At this moment I will exercise the prerogative of tyranny:

"Off with his head!"

I do not believe this person though he have ever so many titles to jingle after his name, nor in the colleges which gave them, if they stand sponsor for that which he writes, I do not believe he has compassed this universe. I believe him to be an inconsequent being like myself--oh, much more learned, of course--and yet only upon the threshold of these wonders. It goes too deep--life--to be solved by fifty years of living. There is far too much in the blue firmament, too many stars, to be dissolved in the feeble logic of a single brain. We are not yet great enough, even this explanatory person, to grasp the "scheme of things entire." This is no place for weak pessimism--this universe. This is Mystery and out of Mystery springs the fine adventure! What we have seen or felt, what we think we know, are insignificant compared with that which may be known.

What this person explains is not, after all, the Universe--but himself, his own limited, faithless personality. I shall not accept his explanation. I escape him utterly!

Not long ago, coming in from my fields, I fell to thinking of the supreme wonder of a tree; and as I walked I met the Professor.

"How," I asked, "does the sap get up to the top of these great maples and elms? What power is there that should draw it upward against the force of gravity?"

He looked at me a moment with his peculiar slow smile.

"I don't know," he said.

"What!" I exclaimed, "do you mean to tell me that science has not solved this simplest of natural phenomena?"

"We do not know," he said. "We explain, but we do not know."

No, my Explanatory Friend, we do not know--we do not know the why of the flowers, or the trees, or the suns; we do not even know why, in our own hearts, we should be asking this curious question--and other deeper questions.

*   *   *   *   *

No man becomes a great writer unless he possesses a highly developed sense of Mystery, of wonder. A great writer is never *blase*; everything to him happened not longer ago than this forenoon.

The other night the Professor and the Scotch Preacher happened in here together and we fell to discussing, I hardly know how, for we usually talk the neighbourhood chat of the Starkweathers, of Horace and of Charles Baxter, we fell to discussing old Izaak Walton--and the nonsense (as a scientific age knows it to be) which he sometimes talked with such delightful sobriety.

"How superior it makes one feel, in behalf of the enlightenment and progress of his age," said the Professor, "when he reads Izaak's extraordinary natural history."

"Does it make you feel that way?" asked the Scotch Preacher. "It makes me want to go fishing."

And he took the old book and turned the leaves until he came to page 54.

"Let me read you," he said, "what the old fellow says about the 'fearfulest of fishes.'"

"'... Get secretly behind a tree, and stand as free from motion as possible; then put a grasshopper on your hook, and let your hook hang a quarter of a yard short of the water, to which end you must rest your rod on some bough of a tree; but it is likely that the Chubs will sink down towards the bottom of the water at the first shadow of your rod, for a Chub is the fearfulest of fishes, and will do so if but a bird flies over him and makes the least shadow on the water; but they will presently rise up to the top again, and there lie soaring until some shadow affrights them again; I say, when they lie upon the top of the water, look at the best Chub, which you, getting yourself in a fit place, may very easily see, and move your rod as slowly as a snail moves, to that Chub you intend to catch, let your bait fall gently upon the water three or four inches before him, and he will infallibly take the bait, and you will be as sure to catch him.... Go your way presently, take my rod, and do as I bid you, and I will sit down and mend my tackling till you return back----'"

"Now I say," said the Scotch Preacher, "that it makes me want to go fishing."

"That," I said, "is true of every great book: it either makes us want to do things, to go fishing, or fight harder or endure more patiently--or it takes us out of ourselves and beguiles us for a time with the friendship of completer lives than our own."

The great books indeed have in them the burning fire of life;

.... "nay, they do preserve, as in a violl, the purest efficacie and extraction of that living intellect that bred them. I know they are as lively, and as vigorously productive, as those fabulous Dragon's teeth; which being sown up and down, may chance to spring up armed men."

How soon we come to distinguish the books of the mere writers from the books of real men! For true literature, like happiness, is ever a by-product; it is the half-conscious expression of a man greatly engaged in some other undertaking; it is the song of one working. There is something inevitable, unrestrainable about the great books; they seemed to come despite the author. "I could not sleep," says the poet Horace, "for the pressure of unwritten poetry." Dante said of his books that they "made him lean for many days." I have heard people say of a writer in explanation of his success:

"Oh, well, he has the literary knack."

It is not so! Nothing is further from the truth. He writes well not chiefly because he is interested in writing, or because he possesses any especial knack, but because he is more profoundly, vividly interested in the activities of life and he tells about them--over his shoulder. For writing, like farming, is ever a tool, not an end.

How the great one-book men remain with us! I can see Marcus Aurelius sitting in his camps among the far barbarians writing out the reflections of a busy life. I see William Penn engaged in great undertakings, setting down "Some of the Fruits of Solitude," and Abraham Lincoln striking, in the hasty paragraphs written for his speeches, one of the highest notes in our American literature.

*   *   *   *   *

"David?"

"Yes, Harriet."

"I am going up now; it is very late."

"Yes."

"You will bank the fire and see that the doors are locked?"

"Yes."

After a pause: "And, David, I didn't mean--about the story you read. Did the Knight finally kill the lions?"

"No," I said with sobriety, "it was not finally necessary."

"But I thought he set out to kill them."

"He did; but he proved his valour without doing it."

Harriet paused, made as if to speak again, but did not do so.

"Valour"--I began in my hortatory tone, seeing a fair opening, but at the look in her eye I immediately desisted.

"You won't stay up late?" she warned.

"N-o," I said.

Take John Bunyan as a pattern of the man who forgot himself into immortality. How seriously he wrote sermons and pamphlets, now happily forgotten! But it was not until he was shut up in jail (some writers I know might profit by his example) that he "put aside," as he said, "a more serious and important work" and wrote "Pilgrim's Progress." It is the strangest thing in the world--the judgment of men as to what is important and serious! Bunyan says in his rhymed introduction:

"I only thought to make I knew not what: nor did I undertake Thereby to please my neighbour; no, not I: I did it my own self to gratify."

Another man I love to have at hand is he who writes of Blazing Bosville, the Flaming Tinman, and of The Hairy Ones.

How Borrow escapes through his books! His object was not to produce literature but to display his erudition as a master of language and of outlandish custom, and he went about the task in all seriousness of demolishing the Roman Catholic

Church. We are not now so impressed with his erudition that we do not smile at his vanity and we are quite contented, even after reading his books, to let the church survive; but how shall we spare our friend with his inextinguishable love of life, his pugilists, his gypsies, his horse traders? We are even willing to plow through arid deserts of dissertation in order that we may enjoy the perfect oases in which the man forgets himself!

Reading such books as these and a hundred others, the books of the worn case at my elbow.

"The bulged and the bruised octavos, The dear and the dumpy twelves----"

I become like those initiated in the Eleusinian mysteries who, as Cicero tells us, have attained "the art of living joyfully and of dying with a fairer hope."

*   *   *   *   *

It is late, and the house is still. A few bright embers glow in the fireplace. You look up and around you, as though coming back to the world from some far-off place. The clock in the dining-room ticks with solemn precision; you did not recall that it had so loud a tone. It has been a great evening, in this quiet room on your farm, you have been able to entertain the worthies of all the past!

You walk out, resoundingly, to the kitchen and open the door. You look across the still white fields. Your barn looms black in the near distance, the white mound close at hand is your wood-pile, the great trees stand like sentinels in the moon-light; snow has drifted upon the doorstep and lies there untracked. It is, indeed, a dim and untracked world: coldly beautiful but silent--and of a strange unreality! You close the door with half a shiver and take the real world with you up to bed. For it is past one o'clock.

XIII
THE POLITICIAN

In the city, as I now recall it (having escaped), it seemed to be the instinctive purpose of every citizen I knew not to get into politics but to keep out. We sedulously avoided caucuses and school-meetings, our time was far too precious to be squandered in jury service, we forgot to register for elections, we neglected to vote. We observed a sort of aristocratic contempt for political activity and then fretted and fumed over the low estate to which our government had fallen--and never saw the humour of it all.

At one time I experienced a sort of political awakening: a "boss" we had was more than ordinarily piratical. I think he had a scheme to steal the city hall and sell the monuments in the park (something of that sort), and I, for one, was disturbed. For a time I really wanted to bear a man's part in helping to correct the abuses, only I did not know how and could not find out.

In the city, when one would learn anything about public matters, he turns, not to life, but to books or newspapers. What we get in the city is not life, but what someone else tells us about life. So I acquired a really formidable row of works on Political Economy and Government (I admire the word "works" in that application) where I found Society laid out for me in the most perfect order--with pennies on its eyes. How often, looking back, I see myself as in those days, read my learned books with a sort of fury of interest!--

From the reading of books I acquired a sham comfort. Dwelling upon the excellent theory of our institutions, I was content to disregard the realities of daily practice. I acquired a mock assurance under which I proceeded complacently to the polls, and cast my vote without knowing a single man on the ticket, what he stood for, or what he really intended to do. The ceremony of the ballot bears to politics much the relationship that the sacrament bears to religion: how often, observing the formality, we yet depart wholly from the spirit of the institution.

It was good to escape that place of hurrying strangers. It was good to get one's feet down into the soil. It was good to be in a place where things *are* because they *grow*, and politics, not less than corn! Oh, my friend, say what you please, argue how you like, this crowding together of men and women in unnatural sur-roundings, this haste to be rich in material things, this attempt to enjoy without production, this removal from first-hand life, is irrational, and the end of it is ruin. If our cities were not recruited constantly with the fresh, clean blood of the coun-try, with boys who still retain some of the power and the vision drawn from the soil, where would they be!

"We're a great people," says Charles Baxter, "but we don't always work at it."

"But we talk about it," says the Scotch Preacher.

"By the way," says Charles Baxter, "have you seen George Warren? He's up for supervisor."

"I haven't yet."

"Well, go around and see him. We must find out exactly what he intends to do with the Summit Hill road. If he is weak on that we'd better look to Matt Devine. At least Matt is safe."

The Scotch Preacher looked at Charles Baxter and said to me with a note of admiration in his voice:

"Isn't this man Baxter getting to be intolerable as a political boss!"

*   *   *   *   *

Baxter's shop! Baxter's shop stands close to the road and just in the edge of a grassy old apple orchard. It is a low, unpainted building, with generous double doors in front, standing irresistibly open as you go by. Even as a stranger coming here first from the city I felt the call of Baxter's shop. Shall I ever forget! It was a still morning--one of those days of warm sunshine--and perfect quiet in the country--and birds in the branches--and apple trees all in bloom. Baxter whistling at his work in the sunlit doorway of his shop, in his long, faded apron, much worn at the knees. He was bending to the rhythmic movement of his plane, and all around him as he worked rose billows of shavings. And oh, the odours of that shop! the fragrant, resinous odour of new-cut pine, the pungent smell of black walnut, the dull odour of oak wood--how they stole out in the sunshine, waylaying you as you came far up the road, beguiling you as you passed the shop, and stealing reproachfully after you as you went onward down the road.

Never shall I forget that grateful moment when I first passed Baxter's shop--a failure from the city--and Baxter looking out at me from his deep, quiet, gray eyes--eyes that were almost a caress!

My wayward feet soon took me, unintroduced, within the doors of that shop, the first of many visits. And I can say no more in appreciation of my ventures there than that I came out always with more than I had when I went in.

The wonders there! The long bench with its huge-jawed wooden vises, and the little dusty windows above looking out into the orchard, and the brown planes and the row of shiny saws, and the most wonderful pattern squares and triangles and curves, each hanging on its own peg; and above, in the rafters, every sort and size of curious wood. And oh! the old bureaus and whatnots and high-boys in the corners waiting their turn to be mended; and the sticky glue-pot waiting, too, on the end of the sawhorse. There is family history here in this shop--no end of it--the small and yet great (because intensely human) tragedies and humours of the long, quiet years among these sunny hills. That whatnot there, the one of black walnut with the top knocked off, that belonged in the old days to----

"Charles Baxter," calls my friend Patterson from the roadway, "can you fix my cupboard?"

"Bring it in," says Charles Baxter, hospitably, and Patterson brings it in, and stops to talk--and stops--and stops--There is great talk in Baxter's shop--the slow-gathered wisdom of the country, the lore of crops and calves and cabinets. In Baxter's shop we choose the next President of these United States!

You laugh! But we do--exactly that. It is in the Baxters' shops (not in Broadway, not in State Street) where the presidents are decided upon. In the little grocery stores you and I know, in the blacksmithies, in the schoolhouses back in the country!

*   *   *   *   *

Forgive me! I did not intend to wander away. I meant to keep to my subject--
but the moment I began to talk of politics in the country I was beset by a compelling
vision of Charles Baxter coming out of his shop in the dusk of the evening, carrying
his curious old reflector lamp and leading the way down the road to the schoolhouse. And thinking of the lamp brought a vision of the joys of Baxter's shop, and
thinking of the shop brought me naturally around to politics and presidents; and
here I am again where I started!

Baxter's lamp is, somehow, inextricably associated in my mind with politics.
Being busy farmers, we hold our caucuses and other meetings in the evening and
usually in the schoolhouse. The schoolhouse is conveniently near to Baxter's shop,
so we gather at Baxter's shop. Baxter takes his lamp down from the bracket above
his bench, reflector and all, and you will see us, a row of dusky figures, Baxter in the
lead, proceeding down the roadway to the schoolhouse. Having arrived, some one
scratches a match, shields it with his hand (I see yet the sudden fitful illumination
of the brown-bearded, watchful faces of my neighbours!) and Baxter guides us into
the schoolhouse--with its shut-in dusty odours of chalk and varnished desks and--
yes, leftover lunches!

Baxter's lamp stands on the table, casting a vast shadow of the chairman on the
wall.

"Come to order," says the chairman, and we have here at this moment in operation the greatest institution in this round world: the institution of free self-government. Great in its simplicity, great in its unselfishness! And Baxter's old lamp with
its smoky tin reflector, is not that the veritable torch of our liberties?

This, I forgot to say, though it makes no special difference--a caucus would be
the same--is a school meeting.

You see, ours is a prolific community. When a young man and a young woman
are married they think about babies; they want babies, and what is more, they have
them! and love them afterward! It is a part of the complete life. And having babies,
there must be a place to teach them to live.

Without more explanation you will understand that we needed an addition to our schoolhouse. A committee reported that the amount required would be $800. We talked it over. The Scotch Preacher was there with a plan which he tacked up on the blackboard and explained to us. He told us of seeing the stone-mason and the carpenter, he told us what the seats would cost, and the door knobs and the hooks in the closet. We are a careful people; we want to know where every penny goes!

"If we put it all in the budget this year what will that make the rate?" inquires a voice from the end of the room.

We don't look around; we know the voice. And when the secretary has computed the rate, if you listen closely you can almost hear the buzz of multiplications and additions which is going on in each man's head as he calculates exactly how much the addition will mean to him in taxes on his farm, his daughter's piano his wife's top-buggy.

And many a man is saying to himself:

"If we build this addition to the schoolhouse, I shall have to give up the new overcoat I have counted upon, or Amanda won't be able to get the new cooking-range."

That's *real* politics: the voluntary surrender of some private good for the up-building of some community good. It is in such exercises that the fibre of democracy grows sound and strong. There is, after all, in this world no real good for which we do not have to surrender something. In the city the average voter is never conscious of any surrender. He never realises that he is giving anything himself for good schools or good streets. Under such conditions how can you expect self-government? No service, no reward!

The first meeting that I sat through watching those bronzed farmers at work gave me such a conception of the true meaning of self-government as I never hoped to have.

"This is the place where I belong," I said to myself.

It was wonderful in that school meeting to see how every essential element of our government was brought into play. Finance? We discussed whether we should put the entire $800 into the next year's budget or divide it paying part in cash and bonding the district for the remainder. The question of credit, of interest, of the obligations of this generation and the next, were all discussed. At one time long ago I was amazed when I heard my neighbours arguing in Baxter's shop about the issuance of certain bonds by the United States government: how completely they understood it! I know now where they got that understanding. Right in the school meetings and town caucuses where they raise money yearly for the expenses of our small government! There is nothing like it in the city.

The progress of a people can best be judged by those things which they accept as matters-of-fact. It was amazing to me, coming from the city, and before I understood, to see how ingrained had become some of the principles which only a few years ago were fiercely-mooted problems. It gave me a new pride in my country, a new appreciation of the steps in civilisation which we have already permanently gained. Not a question have I ever heard in any school meeting of the necessity of educating every American child--at any cost. Think of it! Think how far we have come in that respect, in seventy--yes, fifty--years. Universal education has become a settled axiom of our life.

And there was another point--so common now that we do not appreciate the significance of it. I refer to majority rule. In our school meeting we were voting money out of men's pockets--money that we all needed for private expenses--and yet the moment the minority, after full and honest discussion, failed to maintain its contention in opposition to the new building, it yielded with perfect good humour and went on with the discussion of other questions. When you come to think of it, in the light of history, is not that a wonderful thing?

One of the chief property owners in our neighbourhood is a rather crabbed old bachelor. Having no children and heavy taxes to pay, he looks with jaundiced eye on additions to schoolhouses. He will object and growl and growl and object, and yet pin him down as I have seen the Scotch Preacher pin him more than once, he will admit that children ("of course," he will say, "certainly, of course") must be educated.

"For the good of bachelors as well as other people?" the Scotch Preacher will press it home.

"Certainly, of course."

And when the final issue comes, after full discussion, after he has tried to lop off a few yards of blackboard or order cheaper desks or dispense with the clothes-closet, he votes for the addition with the rest of us.

It is simply amazing to see how much grows out of these discussions--how much of that social sympathy and understanding which is the very tap-root of democracy. It's cheaper to put up a miserable shack of an addition. Why not do it? So we discuss architecture--blindly, it is true; we don't know the books on the subject--but we grope for the big true things, and by our own discussion we educate ourselves to know why a good building is better than a bad one. Heating and ventilation in their relation to health, the use of "fad studies"--how I have heard those things discussed!

How Dr. North, who has now left us forever, shone in those meetings, and Charles Baxter and the Scotch Preacher--broad men, every one--how they have explained and argued, with what patience have they brought into that small schoolhouse, lighted by Charles Baxter's lamp, the grandest conceptions of human society--not in the big words of the books, but in the simple, concrete language of our common life.

"Why teach physiology?"

What a talk Dr. North once gave us on that!

"Why pay a teacher $40 a month when one can be had for $30?"

You should have heard the Scotch Preacher answer that question! Many a one of us went away with some of the education which we had come, somewhat grudgingly, to buy for our children.

These are our political bosses: these unknown patriots, who preach the invisible patriotism which expresses itself not in flags and oratory, but in the quiet daily surrender of private advantage to the public good.

There is, after all, no such thing as perfect equality; there must be leaders, flag-bearers, bosses--whatever you call them. Some men have a genius for leading; others for following; each is necessary and dependent upon the other. In cities, that leadership is often perverted and used to evil ends. Neither leaders nor followers seem to understand. In its essence politics is merely a mode of expressing human sympathy. In the country many and many a leader like Baxter works faithfully year in and year out, posting notices of caucuses, school meetings and elections, opening cold schoolhouses, talking to candidates, prodding selfish voters--and mostly without reward. Occasionally they are elected to petty offices where they do far more work than they are paid for (we have our eyes on 'em); often they are rewarded by the power and place which leadership gives them among their neighbours, and sometimes--and that is Charles Baxter's case--they simply like it! Baxter is of the social temperament: it is the natural expression of his personality. As for thinking of himself as a patriot, he would never dream of it. Work with the hands, close touch with the common life of the soil, has given him much of the true wisdom of experience. He knows us and we know him; he carries the banner, holds it as high as he knows how, and we follow.

Whether there can be a real democracy (as in a city) where there is not that elbow knowledge, that close neighbourhood sympathy, that conscious surrender of little personal goods for bigger public ones, I don't know.

We haven't many foreigners in our district, but all three were there on the night we voted for the addition. They are Polish. Each has a farm where the whole family works--and puts on a little more Americanism each year. They're good people. It is surprising how much all these Poles, Italians, Germans and others, are like us, how perfectly human they are, when we know them personally! One Pole here, named Kausky, I have come to know pretty well, and I declare I have forgotten that he *is* a Pole. There's nothing like the rub of democracy! The reason why we are so suspicious of the foreigners in our cities is that they are crowded together in such vast, unknown, undigested masses. We have swallowed them too fast, and we suffer from a sort of national dyspepsia.

Here in the country we promptly digest our foreigners and they make as good Americans as anybody.

"Catch a foreigner when he first comes here," says Charles Baxter, "and he takes to our politics like a fish to water."

The Scotch Preacher says they "gape for education," And when I see Kausky's six children going by in the morning to school, all their round, sleepy, fat faces shining with soap, I believe it! Baxter tells with humour how he persuaded Kausky to vote for the addition to the schoolhouse. It was a pretty stiff tax for the poor fellow to pay, but Baxter "figgered children with him," as he said. With six to educate, Baxter showed him that he was actually getting a good deal more than he paid for!

Be it far from me to pretend that we are always right or that we have arrived in our country at the perfection of self-government. I do not wish to imply that all of our people are interested, that all attend the caucuses and school-meetings (some of the most prominent never come near--they stay away, and if things don't go right they blame Charles Baxter!) Nor must I over-emphasise the seriousness of our public interest. But we certainly have here, if anywhere in this nation, real self-government. Growth is a slow process. We often fail in our election of delegates to State conventions; we sometimes vote wrong in national affairs. It is an easy thing to think school district; difficult, indeed, to think State or nation. But we grow. When we make mistakes, it is not because we are evil, but because we don't know. Once we get a clear understanding of the right or wrong of any question you can depend upon us--absolutely--to vote for what is right. With more education we shall be able to think in larger and larger circles--until we become, finally, really national in our interests and sympathies. Whenever a man comes along who knows how simple we are, and how much we really want to do right, if we can be convinced that a thing *is* right--who explains how the railroad question, for example, affects us in our intimate daily lives, what the rights and wrongs of it are, why, we can understand and do understand--and we are ready to act.

It is easy to rally to a flag in times of excitement. The patriotism of drums and marching regiments is cheap; blood is material and cheap; physical weariness and hunger are cheap. But the struggle I speak of is not cheap. It is dramatised by few symbols. It deals with hidden spiritual qualities within the conscience of men. Its heroes are yet unsung and unhonoured. No combats in all the world's history were ever fought so high upward in the spiritual air as these; and, surely, not for nothing!

And so, out of my experience both in city and country, I feel--yes, I *know*--that the real motive power of this democracy lies back in the little country neighbourhoods like ours where men gather in dim schoolhouses and practice the invisible patriotism of surrender and service.

XIV
THE HARVEST

"Oh, Universe, what thou wishest, I wish."
                    -- *Marcus Aurelius*

I come to the end of these Adventures with a regret I can scarcely express. I, at least, have enjoyed them. I began setting them down with no thought of publication, but for my own enjoyment; the possibility of a book did not suggest itself until afterwards. I have tried to relate the experiences of that secret, elusive, invisible life which in every man is so far more real, so far more important than his visible activities--the real expression of a life much occupied in other employment.

When I first came to this farm, I came empty-handed. I was the veritable pattern of the city-made failure. I believed that life had nothing more in store for me. I was worn out physically, mentally and, indeed, morally. I had diligently planned for Success; and I had reaped defeat. I came here without plans. I plowed and harrowed and planted, expecting nothing. In due time I began to reap. And it has been a growing marvel to me, the diverse and unexpected crops that I have produced within these uneven acres of earth. With sweat I planted corn, and I have here a crop not only of corn but of happiness and hope. My tilled fields have miraculously sprung up to friends!

This book is one of the unexpected products of my farm. It is this way with the farmer. After the work of planting and cultivating, after the rain has fallen in his fields, after the sun has warmed them, after the new green leaves have broken the earth--one day he stands looking out with a certain new joy across his acres (the wind bends and half turns the long blades of the corn) and there springs up within him a song of the fields. No matter how little poetic, how little articulate he is, the song rises irrepressibly in his heart, and he turns aside from his task with a new glow of fulfillment and contentment. At harvest time in our country I hear, or I imagine I hear, a sort of chorus rising over all the hills, and I meet no man who is not, deep down within him, a singer! So song follows work: so art grows out of life!

And the friends I have made! They have come to me naturally, as the corn grows in my fields or the wind blows in my trees. Some strange potency abides within the soil of this earth! When two men stoop (there must be stooping) and touch it together, a magnetic current is set up between them: a flow of common understanding and confidence. I would call the attention of all great Scientists, Philosophers, and Theologians to this phenomenon: it will repay investigation. It is at once the rarest and the commonest thing I know. It shows that down deep within us, where we really live, we are all a good deal alike. We have much the same instincts, hopes, joys, sorrows. If only it were not for the outward things that we commonly look upon as important (which are in reality not at all important) we might come together without fear, vanity, envy, or prejudice and be friends. And what a world it would be! If civilisation means anything at all it means the increasing ability of men to look through material possessions, through clothing, through differences of speech and colour of skin, and to see the genuine man that abides within each of us. It means an escape from symbols!

I tell this merely to show what surprising and unexpected things have grown out of my farm. All along I have had more than I bargained for. From now on I shall marvel at nothing! When I ordered my own life I failed; now that I work from day to day, doing that which I can do best and which most delights me, I am rewarded in ways that I could not have imagined. Why, it would not surprise me if heaven were at the end of all this!

Now, I am not so foolish as to imagine that a farm is a perfect place. In these Adventures I have emphasised perhaps too forcibly the joyful and pleasant features of my life. In what I have written I have naturally chosen only those things which were most interesting and charming. My life has not been without discouragement and loss and loneliness (loneliness most of all). I have enjoyed the hard work; the little troubles have troubled me more than the big ones. I detest unharnessing a muddy horse in the rain! I don't like chickens in the barn. And somehow Harriet uses an inordinate amount of kindling wood. But once in the habit, unpleasant things have a way of fading quickly and quietly from the memory.

And you see after living so many years in the city the worst experience on the farm is a sort of joy!

In most men as I come to know them--I mean men who dare to look themselves in the eye--I find a deep desire for more naturalness, more directness. How weary we all grow of this fabric of deception which is called modern life. How passionately we desire to escape but cannot see the way! How our hearts beat with sympathy when we find a man who has turned his back upon it all and who says "I will live it no longer." How we flounder in possessions as in a dark and suffocating bog, wasting our energies not upon life but upon *things*. Instead of employing our houses, our cities, our gold, our clothing, we let these inanimate things possess and employ us--to what utter weariness. "Blessed be nothing," sighs a dear old lady of my knowledge.

Of all ways of escape I know, the best, though it is far from perfection, is the farm. There a man may yield himself most nearly to the quiet and orderly processes of nature. He may attain most nearly to that equilibrium between the material and spiritual, with time for the exactions of the first, and leisure for the growth of the second, which is the ideal of life.

In times past most farming regions in this country have suffered the disadvantages of isolation, the people have dwelt far distant from one another and from markets, they have had little to stimulate them intellectually or socially. Strong and peculiar individuals and families were often developed at the expense of a friendly community life: neighbourhood feuds were common. Country life was marked with the rigidity of a hard provincialism. All this, however, is rapidly changing. The closer settlement of the land, the rural delivery of mails (the morning newspaper reaches the tin box at the end of my lane at noon), the farmer's telephone, the spreading country trolleys, more schools and churches, and cheaper railroad rates, have all helped to bring the farmer's life well within the stimulating currents of world thought without robbing it of its ancient advantages. And those advantages are incalculable: Time first for thought and reflection (narrow streams cut deep) leading to the growth of a sturdy freedom of action--which is, indeed, a natural characteristic of the man who has his feet firmly planted upon his own land.

A city hammers and polishes its denizens into a defined model: it worships standardisation; but the country encourages differentiation, it loves new types. Thus it is that so many great and original men have lived their youth upon the land. It would be impossible to imagine Abraham Lincoln brought up in a street of tenements. Family life on the farm is highly educative; there is more discipline for a boy in the continuous care of a cow or a horse than in many a term of school. Industry, patience, perseverance are qualities inherent in the very atmosphere of country life. The so-called manual training of city schools is only a poor makeshift for developing in the city boy those habits which the country boy acquires naturally in his daily life. An honest, hard-working country training is the best inheritance a father can leave his son.

And yet a farm is only an opportunity, a tool. A cornfield, a plow, a woodpile, an oak tree, will cure no man unless he have it in himself to be cured. The truth is that no life, and least of all a farmer's life, is simple--unless it is simple. I know a man and his wife who came out here to the country with the avowed purpose of becoming, forthwith, simple. They were unable to keep the chickens out of their summer kitchen. They discovered microbes in the well, and mosquitoes in the cistern, and wasps in the garret. Owing to the resemblance of the seeds, their radishes turned out to be turnips! The last I heard of them they were living snugly in a flat in Sixteenth Street--all their troubles solved by a dumb-waiter.

The great point of advantage in the life of the country is that if a man is in reality simple, if he love true contentment, it is the place of all places where he can live his life most freely and fully, where he can *grow*. The city affords no such opportunity; indeed, it often destroys, by the seductiveness with which it flaunts its carnal graces, the desire for the higher life which animates every good man.

While on the subject of simplicity it may be well to observe that simplicity does not necessarily, as some of those who escape from the city seem to think, consist in doing without things, but rather in the proper use of things. One cannot return, unless with affectation, to the crudities of a former existence. We do not believe in Diogenes and his tub. Do you not think the good Lord has given us the telephone (that we may better reach that elbow-rub of brotherhood which is the highest of human ideals) and the railroad (that we may widen our human knowledge and sympathy)--and even the motor-car? (though, indeed, I have sometimes imagined that the motor-cars passing this way had a different origin!). He may have given these things to us too fast, faster than we can bear; but is that any reason why we should denounce them all and return to the old, crude, time-consuming ways of our ancestors? I am no reactionary. I do not go back. I neglect no tool of progress. I am too eager to know every wonder in this universe. The motor-car, if I had one, could not carry me fast enough! I must yet fly!

After my experience in the country, if I were to be cross-examined as to the requisites of a farm, I should say that the chief thing to be desired in any sort of agriculture, is good health in the farmer. What, after all, can touch that! How many of our joys that we think intellectual are purely physical! This joy of the morning that the poet carols about so cheerfully, is often nothing more than the exuberance produced by a good hot breakfast. Going out of my kitchen door some mornings and standing for a moment, while I survey the green and spreading fields of my farm, it seems to me truly as if all nature were making a bow to me. It seems to me that there never was a better cow than mine, never a more really perfect horse, and as for pigs, could any in this world herald my approach with more cheerful grunt-ings and squealings!

But there are other requisites for a farm. It must not be too large, else it will keep you away from your friends. Provide a town not too far off (and yet not too near) where you can buy your flour and sell your grain. If there is a railroad con-venient (though not so near that the whistling of the engines reaches you), that is an added advantage. Demand a few good old oak trees, or walnuts, or even elms will do. No well-regulated farm should be without trees; and having secured the oaks--buy your fuel of your neighbours. Thus you will be blessed with beauty both summer and winter.

As for neighbours, accept those nearest at hand; you will find them surprisingly human, like yourself. If you like them you will be surprised to find how much they all like you (and will upon occasion lend you a spring-tooth harrow or a butter tub, or help you with your plowing); but if you hate them they will return your hatred with interest. I have discovered that those who travel in pursuit of better neigh-bours never find them.

Somewhere on every farm, along with the other implements, there should be a row of good books, which should not be allowed to rust with disuse: a book, like a hoe, grows brighter with employment. And no farm, even in this country where we enjoy the even balance of the seasons, rain and shine, shine and rain, should be devoid of that irrigation from the currents of the world's thought which is so essential to the complete life. From the papers which the postman puts in the box flow the true waters of civilisation. You will find within their columns how to be good or how to make pies: you will get out of them what you look for! And finally, down the road from your farm, so that you can hear the bell on Sunday mornings, there should be a little church. It will do you good even though, like me, you do not often attend. It's a sort of Ark of the Covenant; and when you get to it, you will find therein the True Spirit--if you take it with you when you leave home. Of course you will look for good land and comfortable buildings when you buy your farm: they are, indeed, prime requisites. I have put them last for the reason that they are so often first. I have observed, however, that the joy of the farmer is by no means in proportion to the area of his arable land. It is often a nice matter to decide between acres and contentment: men perish from too much as well as from too little. And if it be possible there should be a long table in the dining-room and little chairs around it, and small beds upstairs, and young voices calling at their play in the fields--if it be possible.

Sometimes I say to myself: I have grasped happiness! Here it is; I have it. And yet, it always seems at that moment of complete fulfillment as though my hand trembled, that I might not take it!

I wonder if you recall the story of Christian and Hopeful, how, standing on the hill Clear (as we do sometimes--at our best) they looked for the gates of the Celestial City (as we look--how fondly!):

"Then they essayed to look, but the remembrance of that last thing that the shepherds had showed them made their hands shake, by means of which impediment they could not look steadily through the glass: yet they thought they saw something like the gate, and also some of the glory of the place."

How often I have thought that I saw some of the glory of the place (looking from the hill Clear) and how often, lifting the glass, my hand has trembled!

The Codes Of Hammurabi And Moses
W. W. Davies

QTY

The discovery of the Hammurabi Code is one of the greatest achievements of archaeology, and is of paramount interest, not only to the student of the Bible, but also to all those interested in ancient history...

Religion   **ISBN:** *1-59462-338-4*   **Pages:132**

MSRP $12.95

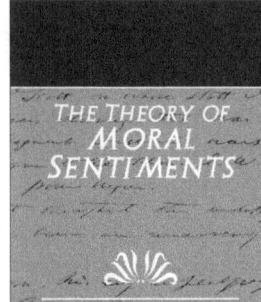

The Theory of Moral Sentiments
Adam Smith

QTY

This work from 1749. contains original theories of conscience amd moral judgment and it is the foundation for systemof morals.

Philosophy   ISBN: *1-59462-777-0*   **Pages:536**

MSRP $19.95

Jessica's First Prayer
Hesba Stretton

QTY

In a screened and secluded corner of one of the many railway-bridges which span the streets of London there could be seen a few years ago, from five o'clock every morning until half past eight, a tidily set-out coffee-stall, consisting of a trestle and board, upon which stood two large tin cans, with a small fire of charcoal burning under each so as to keep the coffee boiling during the early hours of the morning when the work-people were thronging into the city on their way to their daily toil...

Pages:84

Childrens   ISBN: *1-59462-373-2*   *MSRP $9.95*

My Life and Work
Henry Ford

QTY

Henry Ford revolutionized the world with his implementation of mass production for the Model T automobile. Gain valuable business insight into his life and work with his own auto-biography... "We have only started on our development of our country we have not as yet, with all our talk of wonderful progress, done more than scratch the surface. The progress has been wonderful enough but..."

Pages:300

Biographies/   **ISBN:** *1-59462-198-5*   *MSRP $21.95* www.bookjungle.com *email: sales@bookjungle.com fax: 630-214-0564 mail: Book Jungle PO Box 2226 Champaign, IL 61825*

The Art of Cross-Examination
Francis Wellman

QTY

I presume it is the experience of every author, after his first book is published upon an important subject, to be almost overwhelmed with a wealth of ideas and illustrations which could readily have been included in his book, and which to his own mind, at least, seem to make a second edition inevitable. Such certainly was the case with me; and when the first edition had reached its sixth impression in five months, I rejoiced to learn that it seemed to my publishers that the book had met with a sufficiently favorable reception to justify a second and considerably enlarged edition. ..

Pages:412

Reference ISBN: *1-59462-647-2* *MSRP $19.95*

On the Duty of Civil Disobedience
Henry David Thoreau

QTY

Thoreau wrote his famous essay, On the Duty of Civil Disobedience, as a protest against an unjust but popular war and the immoral but popular institution of slave-owning. He did more than write—he declined to pay his taxes, and was hauled off to gaol in consequence. Who can say how much this refusal of his hastened the end of the war and of slavery ?

Law ISBN: *1-59462-747-9* **Pages:48**

MSRP $7.45

Dream Psychology Psychoanalysis for Beginners
Sigmund Freud

QTY

Sigmund Freud, born Sigismund Schlomo Freud (May 6, 1856 - September 23, 1939), was a Jewish-Austrian neurologist and psychiatrist who co-founded the psychoanalytic school of psychology. Freud is best known for his theories of the unconscious mind, especially involving the mechanism of repression; his redefinition of sexual desire as mobile and directed towards a wide variety of objects; and his therapeutic techniques, especially his understanding of transference in the therapeutic relationship and the presumed value of dreams as sources of insight into unconscious desires.

Pages:196

Psychology ISBN: *1-59462-905-6* *MSRP $15.45*

The Miracle of Right Thought
Orison Swett Marden

QTY

Believe with all of your heart that you will do what you were made to do. When the mind has once formed the habit of holding cheerful, happy, prosperous pictures, it will not be easy to form the opposite habit. It does not matter how improbable or how far away this realization may see, or how dark the prospects may be, if we visualize them as best we can, as vividly as possible, hold tenaciously to them and vigorously struggle to attain them, they will gradually become actualized, realized in the life. But a desire, a longing without endeavor, a yearning abandoned or held indifferently will vanish without realization.

Pages:360

Self Help ISBN: *1-59462-644-8* *MSRP $25.45*

The Rosicrucian Cosmo-Conception Mystic Christianity *by Max Heindel*   ISBN: *1-59462-188-8*   **$38.95**
The Rosicrucian Cosmo-conception is not dogmatic, neither does it appeal to any other authority than the reason of the student. It is: not controversial, but is: sent forth in the, hope that it may help to clear...   New Age/Religion Pages 646

Abandonment To Divine Providence *by Jean-Pierre de Caussade*   ISBN: *1-59462-228-0*   **$25.95**
"The Rev. Jean Pierre de Caussade was one of the most remarkable spiritual writers of the Society of Jesus in France in the 18th Century. His death took place at Toulouse in 1751. His works have gone through many editions and have been republished...   Inspirational/Religion Pages 400

Mental Chemistry *by Charles Haanel*   ISBN: *1-59462-192-6*   **$23.95**
Mental Chemistry allows the change of material conditions by combining and appropriately utilizing the power of the mind. Much like applied chemistry creates something new and unique out of careful combinations of chemicals the mastery of mental chemistry...   New Age Pages 354

The Letters of Robert Browning and Elizabeth Barret Barrett 1845-1846 vol II   ISBN: *1-59462-193-4*   **$35.95**
by Robert Browning and Elizabeth Barrett   Biographies Pages 596

Gleanings In Genesis (volume I) *by Arthur W. Pink*   ISBN: *1-59462-130-6*   **$27.45**
Appropriately has Genesis been termed "the seed plot of the Bible" for in it we have, in germ form, almost all of the great doctrines which are afterwards fully developed in the books of Scripture which follow...   Religion/Inspirational Pages 420

The Master Key *by L. W. de Laurence*   ISBN: *1-59462-001-6*   **$30.95**
In no branch of human knowledge has there been a more lively increase of the spirit of research during the past few years than in the study of Psychology, Concentration and Mental Discipline. The requests for authentic lessons in Thought Control, Mental Discipline and...   New Age/Business Pages 422

The Lesser Key Of Solomon Goetia *by L. W. de Laurence*   ISBN: *1-59462-092-X*   **$9.95**
This translation of the first book of the "Lernegton" which is now for the first time made accessible to students of Talismanic Magic was done, after careful collation and edition, from numerous Ancient Manuscripts in Hebrew, Latin, and French...   New Age/Occult Pages 92

Rubaiyat Of Omar Khayyam *by Edward Fitzgerald*   ISBN:*1-59462-332-5*   **$13.95**
Edward Fitzgerald, whom the world has already learned, in spite of his own efforts to remain within the shadow of anonymity, to look upon as one of the rarest poets of the century, was born at Bredfield, in Suffolk, on the 31st of March, 1809. He was the third son of John Purcell...   Music Pages 172

Ancient Law *by Henry Maine*   ISBN: *1-59462-128-4*   **$29.95**
The chief object of the following pages is to indicate some of the earliest ideas of mankind, as they are reflected in Ancient Law, and to point out the relation of those ideas to modern thought.   Religiom/History Pages 452

Far-Away Stories *by William J. Locke*   ISBN: *1-59462-129-2*   **$19.45**
"Good wine needs no bush, but a collection of mixed vintages does. And this book is just such a collection. Some of the stories I do not want to remain buried for ever in the museum files of dead magazine-numbers an author's not unpardonable vanity..."   Fiction Pages 272

Life of David Crockett *by David Crockett*   ISBN: *1-59462-250-7*   **$27.45**
"Colonel David Crockett was one of the most remarkable men of the times in which he lived. Born in humble life, but gifted with a strong will, an indomitable courage, and unremitting perseverance...   Biographies/New Age Pages 424

Lip-Reading *by Edward Nitchie*   ISBN: *1-59462-206-X*   **$25.95**
Edward B. Nitchie, founder of the New York School for the Hard of Hearing, now the Nitchie School of Lip-Reading, Inc, wrote "LIP-READING Principles and Practice". The development and perfecting of this meritorious work on lip-reading was an undertaking...   How-to Pages 400

A Handbook of Suggestive Therapeutics, Applied Hypnotism, Psychic Science   ISBN: *1-59462-214-0*   **$24.95**
by Henry Munro   Health/New Age/Health/Self-help Pages 376

A Doll's House: and Two Other Plays *by Henrik Ibsen*   ISBN: *1-59462-112-8*   **$19.95**
Henrik Ibsen created this classic when in revolutionary 1848 Rome. Introducing some striking concepts in playwriting for the realist genre, this play has been studied the world over.   Fiction/Classics/Plays 308

The Light of Asia *by sir Edwin Arnold*   ISBN: *1-59462-204-3*   **$13.95**
In this poetic masterpiece, Edwin Arnold describes the life and teachings of Buddha. The man who was to become known as Buddha to the world was born as Prince Gautama of India but he rejected the worldly riches and abandoned the reigns of power when...   Religion/History/Biographies Pages 170

The Complete Works of Guy de Maupassant *by Guy de Maupassant*   ISBN: *1-59462-157-8*   **$16.95**
"For days and days, nights and nights, I had dreamed of that first kiss which was to consecrate our engagement, and I knew not on what spot I should put my lips..."   Fiction/Classics Pages 240

The Art of Cross-Examination *by Francis L. Wellman*   ISBN: *1-59462-309-0*   **$26.95**
Written by a renowned trial lawyer, Wellman imparts his experience and uses case studies to explain how to use psychology to extract desired information through questioning.   How-to/Science/Reference Pages 408

Answered or Unanswered? *by Louisa Vaughan*   ISBN: *1-59462-248-5*   **$10.95**
Miracles of Faith in China   Religion Pages 112

The Edinburgh Lectures on Mental Science (1909) *by Thomas*   ISBN: *1-59462-008-3*   **$11.95**
This book contains the substance of a course of lectures recently given by the writer in the Queen Street Hail, Edinburgh. Its purpose is to indicate the Natural Principles governing the relation between Mental Action and Material Conditions...   New Age/Psychology Pages 148

Ayesha *by H. Rider Haggard*   ISBN: *1-59462-301-5*   **$24.95**
Verily and indeed it is the unexpected that happens! Probably if there was one person upon the earth from whom the Editor of this, and of a certain previous history, did not expect to hear again...   Classics Pages 380

Ayala's Angel *by Anthony Trollope*   ISBN: *1-59462-352-X*   **$29.95**
The two girls were both pretty, but Lucy who was twenty-one who supposed to be simple and comparatively unattractive, whereas Ayala was credited, as her Bombwhat romantic name might show, with poetic charm and a taste for romance. Ayala when her father died was nineteen...   Fiction Pages 484

The American Commonwealth *by James Bryce*   ISBN: *1-59462-286-8*   **$34.45**
An interpretation of American democratic political theory. It examines political mechanics and society from the perspective of Scotsman James Bryce   Politics Pages 572

Stories of the Pilgrims *by Margaret P. Pumphrey*   ISBN: *1-59462-116-0*   **$17.95**
This book explores pilgrims religious oppression in England as well as their escape to Holland and eventual crossing to America on the Mayflower, and their early days in New England...   History Pages 268

www.bookjungle.com *email: sales@bookjungle.com fax: 630-214-0564 mail: Book Jungle PO Box 2226 Champaign, IL 61825*

QTY

The Fasting Cure *by Sinclair Upton*   ISBN: *1-59462-222-1* **$13.95**

In the Cosmopolitan Magazine for May, 1910, and in the Contemporary Review (London) for April, 1910, I published an article dealing with my experiences in fasting. I have written a great many magazine articles, but never one which attracted so much attention... New Age/Self Help/Health Pages 164

Hebrew Astrology *by Sepharial*   ISBN: *1-59462-308-2* **$13.45**

In these days of advanced thinking it is a matter of common observation that we have left many of the old landmarks behind and that we are now pressing forward to greater heights and to a wider horizon than that which represented the mind-content of our progenitors... Astrology Pages 144

Thought Vibration or The Law of Attraction in the Thought World   ISBN: *1-59462-127-6* **$12.95**

by William Walker Atkinson   *Psychology/Religion Pages 144*

Optimism *by Helen Keller*   ISBN: *1-59462-108-X* **$15.95**

Helen Keller was blind, deaf, and mute since 19 months old, yet famously learned how to overcome these handicaps, communicate with the world, and spread her lectures promoting optimism. An inspiring read for everyone... Biographies/Inspirational Pages 84

Sara Crewe *by Frances Burnett*   ISBN: *1-59462-360-0* **$9.45**

In the first place, Miss Minchin lived in London. Her home was a large, dull, tall one, in a large, dull square, where all the houses were alike, and all the sparrows were alike, and where all the door-knockers made the same heavy sound... Childrens/Classic Pages 88

The Autobiography of Benjamin Franklin *by Benjamin Franklin*   ISBN: *1-59462-135-7* **$24.95**

The Autobiography of Benjamin Franklin has probably been more extensively read than any other American historical work, and no other book of its kind has had such ups and downs of fortune. Franklin lived for many years in England, where he was agent... Biographies/History Pages 332

Name	
Email	
Telephone	
Address	
City, State ZIP	

☐ **Credit Card**   ☐ **Check / Money Order**

Credit Card Number	
Expiration Date	
Signature	

Please Mail to: Book Jungle
PO Box 2226
Champaign, IL 61825
or Fax to: 630-214-0564

ORDERING INFORMATION

web: *www.bookjungle.com*
email: *sales@bookjungle.com*
fax: *630-214-0564*
mail: *Book Jungle PO Box 2226 Champaign, IL 61825*
or PayPal *to sales@bookjungle.com*

Please contact us for bulk discounts

DIRECT-ORDER TERMS

**20% Discount if You Order
Two or More Books**

Free Domestic Shipping!
Accepted: Master Card, Visa,
Discover, American Express